"It is kind of you to show concern, Detective King."

"Please, call me Samuel."

"Samuel." Her soft voice drew his attention. "Who are you, Samuel? You dress like an Amish man. Our men are not detectives." Her eyes studied him.

"I assure you, Sarah, I am a detective. I was raised Amish. I left my home in Ohio and joined the police force about fifteen years ago."

"You are very far from home, aren't you?" she asked.

"I wanted to get as far away as I could." Sam shrugged. "Memories aren't always good."

Her eyes shimmered, and he fought not to lose himself in their beauty.

"I wish I had some memories," she whispered.

"Memories aren't all they're cracked up to be, Sarah. I have memories, but no one to love me. You don't have memories, but you have people who love you very much."

Her beauty spoke to him, stirring feelings better left dormant. Stepping back, he reminded himself of his own rules.

Books by Diane Burke

Love Inspired Suspense

Midnight Caller
Double Identity
Bounty Hunter Guardian
Silent Witness
Hidden in Plain View

DIANE BURKE

is the mother of three grown sons and the grandmother of five grandsons and three step-grandchildren. She has three daughters-in-law who have blessed her by their addition to her family. She lives in Florida, nestled somewhere between the Daytona Beach speedway and the St. Augustine fort, with Cocoa, her golden Lab, and Thea, her border collie. Thea and Cocoa don't know they are dogs, because no one has ever told them. Shhh.

When she was growing up, her siblings always believed she could "exaggerate" her way through any story and often waited with bated breath to see how events turned out, even though they had been present at most of them. Now she brings those stories to life on the written page.

Her writing has earned her numerous awards, including a Daphne du Maurier Award of Excellence.

She would love to hear from her readers. You can contact her at diane@dianeburkeauthor.com.

HIDDEN IN PLAIN VIEW

DIANE BURKE

HARLEQUIN® LOVE INSPIRED® SUSPENSE

Recycling programs
for this product may
not exist in your area.

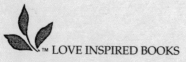 **™ LOVE INSPIRED BOOKS**

ISBN-13: 978-0-373-44535-6

HIDDEN IN PLAIN VIEW

www.LoveInspiredBooks.com

Printed in U.S.A.

Don't be afraid, for I am with you.
Don't be discouraged, for I am your God.
I will strengthen you and help you.
I will hold you up with my victorious right hand.
—*Isaiah* 41:10

This book is dedicated to the family and friends who offered nothing but love and open arms to both my son and me during our long-overdue reunion.

I also wish to thank Rachel Burkot, my new editor, for jumping in midstream and doing a phenomenal job of helping me make this book the best it could be.

PROLOGUE

Mount Hope, Lancaster County, PA

Sarah Lapp wasn't thinking about guns or violence or murder on this unseasonably warm fall day. She was thinking about getting her basket of apples and cheese to the schoolhouse.

Pedaling her bicycle down the dirt road, she spotted the silhouettes of her in-laws, Rebecca and Jacob, standing close together in the distant field.

Sarah knew when she'd married their son, Peter, that she had been fortunate to have married her best friend.

But sometimes…

She glanced at them again.

Sometimes she couldn't help but wonder what true love felt like.

Chiding herself for her foolish notions, she turned her attention back to the road. A sense of unease taunted her as she approached the school. The children should be out in the yard on their first break of the day, but the ball field was empty.

She hit the kickstand on her bike and looked around the yard.

Peter's horse and wagon were tethered to the rail, a

water bucket beside them. Children's bicycles haphazardly dotted the lawn. The bats for the morning ball game rested against the bottom of the steps.

Everything appeared normal.

But it didn't *feel* normal.

Sarah climbed the steps and moved cautiously across the small landing, noting the open windows and the curtains fluttering in the breeze.

Silence.

Her pulse pounded. *When was a room full of children ever silent?*

She'd barely turned the knob when the door was pulled wide with such force that Sarah was propelled forward and sprawled across the floor.

Peter started in her direction.

"Stop right there, Peter, unless you want to see your wife hurt." The speaker was John Zook, a cousin who had recently returned to the Amish way of life. He pulled Sarah roughly to her feet.

"John?" Sarah gasped when she saw a gun peeking out from the folds of the carpentry apron tied around his waist.

Immediately Peter and the teacher, Hannah, gathered the children together and took a protective stance in front of them, shielding their view of the room.

Sarah stood alone in the middle of the room and faced the gunman. She saw fear in his hooded eyes—fear and something else. Something hard and cold.

"John, why are you doing this terrible thing?" she asked.

"Is he out there? Did you see him?"

"Who, John? Who do you think is out there?" Sarah tried to understand what was frightening him.

"What do you want?" Peter's voice commanded from the back of the room.

"I want you to shut up," John snapped in return.

Sarah glanced at the children and marveled at how well behaved and silent they were. John had made sure the adults had seen his weapon, but Sarah was fairly certain the children had not. They seemed more confused and curious than frightened.

John lifted the curtain. "He's out there. I know it."

"John, I did not pass anyone on the road. It was just me." Sarah kept her voice calm and friendly. "We will help you if you will tell us what it is that frightens you so."

When John looked at them, Sarah was taken aback by the absolute terror she saw in his eyes. "He's going to kill me," he whispered. "There will be no place I can hide."

Peter, his patience running thin, yelled at the man. "You are starting to scare the children. I am going to let them out the back door and send them home."

"Nobody moves," John ordered.

Feeling the tension escalate, Sarah tried to find words to defuse the situation. "Peter is right. Whatever's wrong, we will help you. But you must let the children leave."

John shot a furtive glance at the group huddled in the corner and then nodded. "All right. Get them out of here, but make it quick."

Peter ushered the children outside, with whispers to each child to run straight home. When the teacher came up behind the last child, Peter ignored her protests and shoved her to safety, too.

John shoved a felt pouch at Sarah. "Hide this and don't give it to anyone but me. Understand?"

The heavy and cumbersome bag felt like rocks or marbles were nestled inside. She used several straight pins to bind it to her waistband.

Suddenly the sound of boots pounding against the wooden steps filled the air.

"Shut up. Don't make a sound!" John ordered. With trembling hands, he aimed his gun and waited for the door to open. But it didn't.

Instead, bullets slammed *through* the door.

"Sarah, get down!" Peter yelled from across the room.

Pieces of wood from the walls and desks, as well as chunks of chalkboard, splintered as each bullet reached a target.

John Zook grabbed his shoulder. Then doubled over and clutched his stomach, groaning in pain.

The door banged open and slammed against the wall. A stranger entered, this one much taller, with darkness in his eyes that cemented Sarah's feet to the floor in fear.

"Hello, John. Didn't expect to see me, did you?"

The slighter man's body shook. "I was gonna call and let you know where I was, Jimmy. Just as soon as I found a safe place for us to hide out."

"Is that so? Well, I saved you the trouble. Give me my diamonds."

Diamonds?

Instantly, Sarah's fingers flew to the pouch hidden in the folds of her skirt.

"You've got until the count of three. One."

"I don't have them. I have to go get them."

"Two."

"I don't have them!" John's voice came out in an almost hysterical pitch.

"Please, Jimmy, honest." John pulled Sarah in front of him. "She has them. I gave them to her."

Sarah looked into the stranger's face, and evil looked back.

"Three."

The sudden burst of gunfire shook Sarah to her core. A small, round hole appeared in John's forehead. His expression registered surprise and his hand, which had been painfully gripping Sarah's arm, opened. He fell to the floor.

The loud, piercing sound of a metal triangle rent the air. The children had reached their homes. Help was on the way.

The shooter leered at Sarah. "Let's take a look and see what you're hiding in that skirt, shall we?"

"No!" Peter yelled, and ran toward her.

The intruder fired.

Her husband's body jerked not once but twice as he grabbed his chest and collapsed in a heap on the floor.

"Peter!"

Sarah's heart refused to accept what her mind knew was fact. Peter was dead.

Before she could drop to his side, something slammed into the left side of her head. Another blow to her arm. To her back. Pain seized her breath. Weakened her knees. Crumpled her to the floor.

She stretched her right arm out toward Peter, their fingers almost touching as she slid into blessed oblivion.

ONE

Where am I?

Sarah Lapp lay on a bed with raised metal rails. She noted a darkened television screen bracketed to the opposite wall. A nightstand and recliner beside the bed.

I'm in a hospital.

She tried to sit up but couldn't. She was hooked up to machines. Lots of them. Fear pumped her heart into overdrive.

Why am I here?

Again she tried to move, but her body screamed in protest.

Burning pain. Throbbing pain.

Searing the skin on her back. Pulsing through her arm and gathering behind her eyes.

She tried to raise her left arm to touch her forehead but it felt heavy, weighted down, lost in its own gnawing sea of hurt. She glanced down and saw it bandaged and held against her chest by a blue cloth sling.

I've injured my arm. But how? Why can't I remember? And why do I feel so scared?

She took a deep breath.

Don't panic. Take your time. Think.

Once more she inhaled, held it for a second, and forced

herself to ever so slowly release it. Repeating the process a couple more times helped her regain a sense of calm.

Okay. She could do this.

She opened her eyes and stared into the darkness.

"Sarah?"

Sarah? Is that my name?

Why can't I remember?

Her heart almost leaped from her chest when one of the shadows moved.

The man had been leaning against the wall. She hadn't seen him standing in the shadows until he stepped forward. He obviously wasn't a doctor. His garb seemed familiar yet somehow different. He wore black boots, brown pants held up with suspenders and a white shirt with the sleeves rolled to his elbows. He carried a straw hat.

"I thought I heard you stirring." He approached her bed and leaned on the side rail. She found the deep timbre of his voice soothing.

The faint glow from the overhead night-light illuminated his features. She stared at his clean-shaven face, the square jaw, the tanned skin, his intense brown eyes. She searched for some form of recognition but found none.

"I'm glad you're awake." He smiled down at her.

She tried to speak but could only make hoarse, croaking sounds.

"Here, let me get you something to drink." He pushed a button, which raised the head of her bed. He lifted a cup and held it to her lips. There was something intimate and kind in the gesture, and although she didn't recognize this man, she welcomed his presence.

Gratefully, she took a sip, enjoying the soothing coolness of the liquid as it slid over her parched lips and trickled down her throat. When he moved the cup away, she tried again.

"Who…who are you?"

His large hand gently cupped her fingers. She found the warmth of his touch comforting. His brown shaggy hair brushed the collar of his shirt. Tiny lines crinkled the skin at the sides of his eyes.

"My name is Samuel, and I'm here to help you."

Her throat felt like someone had shredded her vocal cords. Her mouth was so dry that even after the sip of water, she couldn't gather enough saliva for a good spit. When she did speak, her voice reflected the strain in a hoarse, barely audible whisper.

"Where… What…" She struggled to force the words out.

"You're in a hospital. You've been shot."

Shot!

No wonder she had felt so afraid when he'd moved out of the shadows. She might not remember the incident, but some inner instinct was still keeping her alert and wary of danger.

"Can you tell me what you remember?" There was kindness in his eyes and an intensity that she couldn't identify.

She shook her head.

"Do you remember being in the schoolhouse when the gunman entered? Did you get a good look at him?"

Schoolhouse? Gunman?

Her stomach lurched, and she thought she was going to be sick. Slowly, she moved her head back and forth again.

"How about before the shooting? Your husband was inside the building constructing bookshelves. Do you remember bringing a basket of treats for the children?"

His words caused a riotous tumble of questions in her mind. She had a husband? Who was he? *Where* was he? She tried to focus her thoughts. This man just told her she'd been shot inside a school. Had anyone else been hurt? Hopefully, none of the children.

"Hus…husband?"

"Sarah. There's no easy way to tell you. Your husband was killed in the shooting."

The room started to spin. Sarah squeezed her eyes shut.

"I'm so sorry. I wish there had been an easier way to break the news." His deep, masculine voice bathed her senses with sympathy and helped her remain calm. "I hate to have to question you right now, but time is of the essence." The feel of his breath on her cheek told her he had stepped closer. "I need you to tell me what you remember—what you saw that day, before things other people tell you cloud your memories."

A lone tear escaped and coursed its way down her cheek at the irony of it all.

"Can you tell me anything about that day?" he prodded. "Sometimes the slightest detail that you might think is unimportant can turn into a lead. If you didn't see the shooter's face, can you remember his height? The color of his skin? What he wore? Anything he might have said?"

He paused, giving her time to collect her thoughts, but only moments later the questions came again.

"If you don't remember seeing anything, use your other senses. Did you hear anything? Smell anything?"

She opened her eyes and stared into his. "I told you." She choked back a sob. "I can't…can't remember. I can't remember anything at all."

His wrinkled brow and deep frown let her know this wasn't what he had expected.

"Maybe you should rest now. I'll be back, and we can talk more later."

Sarah watched him cross to the door. Once he was

gone, she stared at her hand and wondered why the touch of a stranger had made her feel so safe.

Sam stood in the corridor and tried to collect his thoughts.

Sarah.

He hadn't expected to be so touched by her unfortunate circumstances. He had a policy to never let emotions play a part when he was undercover or protecting a witness. Sarah Lapp was a job, nothing more, and he had no business feeling anything for her one way or the other.

But he had to admit there was something about her. He'd been moved by the vulnerability he saw in her face, the fear he read in her eyes. She was terrified. Yet she had stayed calm, processing everything he had to tell her with quiet grace.

She'd been visibly upset when Sam had told her about the shooting. She'd seemed shocked when he informed her that her husband had been killed. But learning that she had had a husband at all seemed to affect her the most.

He hadn't had an opportunity yet to talk with Sarah's doctors about the full extent of her injuries. Was she really suffering from memory loss, and if so, was it a temporary setback or a permanent situation?

Sam often relied heavily on his gut. His instincts this time were warning him that he had just stepped into a much more complicated situation than he had first thought.

He needed to talk with the doctor.

When he glanced down the hall, he saw Dr. Clark, as well as several members of the police force, including his superior, with three Amish men in tow. Dr. Clark ushered the entire group into a nearby conference room and gestured for Sam to join them.

Once inside, Sam crossed the room and leaned against

the far wall. He saw the men shoot furtive glances his way and knew they were confused by his Amish clothing.

He didn't blame them. He was disconcerted by it, too. He hadn't donned this type of clothing for fifteen years. Yet his fingers never hesitated when he fastened the suspenders. The straw hat had rested upon his head like it was meant to be there.

Jacob Lapp, identifying himself as the bishop of their community and acting as spokesperson for their group, addressed Captain Rogers.

"We do not understand, sir. Why have you brought us here?"

"Please, gentlemen, have a seat." Captain Rogers gestured toward the chairs around the table. "Dr. Clark wants to update you on Sarah's condition."

They pulled out chairs and sat down.

Dr. Clark spoke from his position at the head of the table. "Sarah is in a very fragile state. She was shot twice in the back, once in the arm and once in the head. She has a long road to recovery, but I believe she *will* recover. To complicate matters, she is suffering from amnesia."

"Will her memory return?" Jacob asked.

"I'm afraid I honestly don't know. Only time will tell."

The man on Jacob's left spoke. "Excuse me, sir. My name is Benjamin Miller. I do not understand this thing you call amnesia. I had a neighbor who got kicked in the head by his mule. He forgot what happened with his mule, but he didn't forget everything else. He still remembered who he was, who his family was. Why can't Sarah?"

The doctor smiled. "It is common for a person not to remember a traumatic event but to remember everything else. What is less common, but still occurs, is a deeper memory loss. Some people forget everything— like Sarah."

"When she gets better, she will remember again, *ya?*" Jacob twirled his black felt hat in circles on the table.

"I hope that once she returns home, familiar surroundings will help, but I cannot promise anything," the doctor replied.

The men looked at each other and nodded.

"There is something else. Sarah is sixteen weeks pregnant."

Sam felt like someone had suddenly punched him in the gut. Wow, this woman couldn't catch a break. As if amnesia, gunshot wounds and widowhood wasn't enough for her to handle. He raised an eyebrow, but steeled himself to show no other reaction to the news.

The doctor waited for the men at the table to digest the information before he locked eyes with Jacob. "Mrs. Lapp has informed me that Sarah has had two prior miscarriages."

Jacob nodded but remained silent. The information regarding this pregnancy seemed to weigh heavily upon him.

"I'm sorry to inform you, Mr. Lapp, that even though she has made it into her second trimester, she still might lose the child. She has experienced severe trauma to her body, and currently she is under emotional stress as well."

"With my son gone, this will be our only grandchild." Jacob's eyes clouded over. "What can we do to help?"

"You can allow me to protect her." Sam pushed away from the wall and approached the table.

The bishop's expression revealed his confusion. "Protect Sarah? I don't understand, sir. The man who hurt Sarah is gone, *ya?* She is safe now." Jacob looked directly at Sam. "Excuse me, sir. We do not recognize you. What community do you call home?"

Captain Rogers nodded permission for Sam to answer the questions.

"My name is Detective Samuel King. Standing to my left is my partner, Detective Masterson. To his right is Special Agent Lopez from the FBI. We believe Sarah is in grave danger."

"From whom?" Benjamin spoke up, gesturing with his arm to the men sitting on either side of him. "Her family? Her friends?"

Sam addressed his words to Bishop Lapp. "Since I was raised Amish, Captain Rogers thought it might be easier for me to blend in with your community as Sarah's protective detail."

All three men gasped, then turned and whispered in their native Pennsylvania German dialect commonly known as Pennsylvania Dutch.

Sam understood not only the words, but also the emotions and objections the men were expressing. The Amish do not care for law enforcement and try to keep themselves separate from the *Englisch* way of life.

"With respect, sir," Jacob said, "although grateful, we do not feel we need your protection, and neither does Sarah."

Sam sighed heavily. "You are wrong." When he had their full attention, he said, "If you do not allow us to help, Sarah will be dead before this week is over, as well as her unborn child and many of the kids who were inside that schoolhouse when the shooting occurred."

Samuel noted the sudden pallor in Jacob's face. He recognized bewilderment in the other men's eyes and glimpsed hesitation in their body language, but they continued to listen.

Sam pulled out a chair and faced the men. He explained about the diamond heist and the murders of the other thieves, which led to the shoot-out in the school.

Matthew Kauffman, the third Amish man in the group, spoke up for the first time. "If you were once Amish, then you know that we cannot allow police to move into our homes. It is not our way."

"I understand your dilemma," Sam responded. "I assure you that although I left my Amish roots behind, I never abandoned my respect for the Amish ways."

"You do not speak like us," Benjamin insisted. "You sound like an *Englischer.*"

Sam slipped easily into the lilt of the Pennsylvania Dutch dialect. "Many years of living with the *Englisch,* and you can start to sound like one, ain't so?"

"Why did you leave your home, sir?" Benjamin asked.

Sam took a moment to decide just how much he was willing to share with these men.

"In my youth, I witnessed too many things for a young boy to see. I witnessed theft of Amish goods that went unpunished. I witnessed bullying and cruelty against the Amish people, yet I could not raise my hand to retaliate."

The men nodded.

"I witnessed worse. I witnessed drunken teens race their car into my father's buggy just for the fun of it. My parents did not survive their prank."

Several heartbeats of silence filled the room as everyone present absorbed what he'd said.

"The Amish forgive." Sam shrugged. "I could not. So I left."

"It is difficult sometimes to forgive, to not seek vengeance and to move on with life." Jacob's quiet voice held empathy. His eyes seemed to understand that Sam's emotional wounds had not healed and still cut deep. "I understand how hard it can be. I just lost my only son. But…"

He looked Sam straight in the eye. "It is not our place to judge." When he spoke, his voice was soft and sad. "Judgment belongs only to God, *ya?*"

"And vengeance belongs to the Lord, not us," Benjamin Miller added.

"I am not talking about vengeance," Sam said, defending himself. "I am talking about justice."

Jacob scrutinized Sam as if he were trying to determine his character from his words. "How do you know whether what you call justice, Detective King, is what God would call vengeance? Is it not best to leave these matters in God's hands?"

A sad ghost of a smile twisted Sam's lips. "I believe God intended for us to love one another, to help one another. I believe He expects us to protect those who cannot protect themselves. Children. Unborn babies. An innocent woman who doesn't even know the gravity of her loss yet. Isn't that God's will?"

Jacob remained silent and pensive.

Sam had to work hard to control his emotions. There was no place in police work, particularly undercover police work, to let emotions control your actions or thoughts. But he understood these people. He'd been one of them. He knew they were pacifists who refused to fight back. If a gunman walked up and shot them dead on the street, they'd believe it was God's will.

How was he going to make them understand the danger they were in? Or worse, defend against that danger? Jacob was their bishop. He was the one he had to win over. Sam knew the only hope he had of convincing Lapp to go along with the plan was to drive home the pain the man was still feeling from his loss. He challenged him with a hard stare.

"Are you willing to accept responsibility for the deaths

of your loved ones, Bishop? Your neighbors' loved ones?
To never see your grandchild? To attend the funerals of
your neighbors' children? Because you will be killing
them just as if you held the gun and shot them yourself."

Sam's voice had a hardened edge, but he made no apol-
ogies for his harshness. He had to make these men understand the seriousness of the situation if he stood any
chance of saving their lives.

"Please, sir, listen to me," he continued. "A stranger
entered your Amish schoolhouse on a beautiful, peaceful spring afternoon. He cared only about diamonds, not
about God or the sanctity of life." Sam placed his forearms on the table and leaned closer. "This isn't his first
crime. We suspect him of many other crimes, but have
been unable to bring him to justice.

"No one who would be able to describe him has lived
to talk about it—except Sarah. Don't be fooled. He will
return. He will find a way to walk freely among you. He
is not above using your children—perhaps killing your
children—to accomplish his goals. You will never sense
the danger until it is too late."

The three men shot concerned glances at one another.

"Please," Sam pleaded. "Even *with* your help, we cannot
promise that he won't succeed. We are chasing a shadow."

Sam paused, letting the men absorb his words. He gestured toward the other law-enforcement officers in the
room.

"We are not asking you to take up arms or fight back.
But we cannot protect you from the outside alone. If we
stand any chance of stopping this man, then we must be
close. We must be on the inside. We are asking for your
help."

Jacob's head bent, and his lips moved in silent prayer.

After a few moments of silence, he wiped a tear from his cheek and turned to the other Amish men.

"How can we not help?" he asked. "This is our Sarah. Hasn't she been hurt enough? These are our children he speaks of. Is it not our duty as parents to protect them? And what of the innocent child Sarah carries? Must we not protect that child, too?"

"Jacob, you know if this horrible thing he speaks of happens, then it is the will of God." Benjamin's voice was insistent. "We must accept the will of God."

Jacob nodded slowly. "*Ya,* Benjamin, you are right. We must accept the will of God." After a moment, he made eye contact with Benjamin. "Your Mary was in that classroom…and your Daniel and William." Jacob glanced from him to the other man. "Matthew, your children, Emma, Joseph, John, Amos…they were there that terrible day, too." His eyes implored both men. "Are we so eager to let the wolf snatch them away that we stand aside and open the door?"

Benjamin blanched as the realization of what was at stake finally hit him. Visibly shaken, he lowered his head, his voice almost a whisper. "But if it is God's will…"

"I agree. We must accept God's will." Jacob leaned forward and placed his hand on his friend's shoulder. "But I have to ask you, Benjamin, how many detectives do we know who used to be Amish? Maybe sending Samuel to us *is* the will of God."

The men exchanged looks, whispered together in hushed tones and then nodded their heads.

This time, Jacob looked directly at the police captain. "We will agree to this. But please, sir, find the man you seek quickly. We cannot endure this situation for long."

The captain stood and thanked the men for their cooperation. "We will be placing undercover officers in your town. They will deliver your mail, pick up your milk and serve in your local shops and restaurants. But only one will actually enter your home—Detective Samuel King."

Sam hadn't been back on Amish soil for more than a decade. He'd have to keep his emotions in check, his mind clear and his thoughts logical. A woman's life, and that of her unborn child, were at stake. The gravity of the situation weighed heavily on his shoulders, and he prayed he'd be up to the challenge.

TWO

Sarah stared out the window. It had been one week since the shootings, two days since she'd awakened in this hospital room and they still hadn't caught the shooter.

She watched the people below in the parking lot.

Was he out there? Waiting? Plotting? Biding his time like a poisonous snake in the grass, coiled and ready to strike?

Would he come back for her? And if he did, this time…

Sarah didn't have to remember the past to know that she had no desire to die in the present.

She studied the men passing beneath her window. Did any of them look up in her direction? Was the killer watching her even now?

Fear shuddered through her.

How could she protect herself when she didn't even know what the man who posed a threat looked like? How could she help the police catch him before he could hurt more people if her mind continued to be nothing more than a blank slate?

Her mother-in-law, Rebecca, and the doctor had filled her in on what they knew of the details of that day.

The story they had told her was tragic. But she had no emotional connection to that schoolroom, or to the children who had fled out the back door and summoned help, or, even worse, to the man who had once shared her life and was now dead and buried.

She knew people expected an emotional response from her—tears, at least—but she felt nothing.

Surprise? Yes.

Empathy? Of course.

Pain? Grief?

No. They were the emotions she saw every time she looked at the sadness etched in Rebecca's face. She had lost a son.

Sarah had lost a stranger.

Earlier Rebecca had told Sarah that she'd been raised *Englisch* until the age of eight. Try as she might, she couldn't find any memory of those childhood years.

Following her mother's death, she'd been adopted by her Amish grandmother, who had also passed on years ago. Then she'd come to live with Jacob and Rebecca, embraced the Amish faith and married their son. Sarah found it more difficult to come to terms with the person she was supposed to be than to try to summon grief she couldn't feel.

She was a pregnant Amish widow recovering from multiple gunshot wounds and suffering from amnesia. That was her reality. That was the only world to which she could relate.

She couldn't conjure up the slightest recollection of Peter Lapp. Had he been of average build? Or was he tall? Had he had blond hair like his mother? Or maybe brown?

Rebecca had told her they'd been married five years and were happy together.

Had they been happy together? Were they still as much in love on the day of his death as they'd been the day they married? She hoped so. But can true love be forgotten as easily as a breath of air on a spring day? If they'd been soul mates, shouldn't she feel *something*? Have some sense of loss deep in her being, even if she couldn't remember the features of his face or the color of his hair?

Rebecca had also told her that she'd had two prior miscarriages. Had Sarah told her husband about this pregnancy? Were they happy about this blessing or anxious and fearful that it, too, would fail?

A surge of emotion stole her breath away. It wasn't grief. It was anger.

She wanted to be able to grieve for her husband. She wanted to be able to miss him, to shed tears for *him*. Instead, all she felt was guilt for not remembering the man. Not the sound of his voice. Not the feel of his touch. Not even the memory of his face. What kind of wife was she that a man who had shared her life was nothing more to her now than a story on someone else's lips?

She was no longer a complete human being. She was nothing more than an empty void and had nothing within to draw upon. No feelings for her dead husband. No feelings for an unborn child she hadn't even known she carried. No memories of what kind of person she had been. She was broken, damaged goods and of no use to anyone.

Please, God, help me. Please let me climb out of this dark and frightening place.

In the stillness of her empty room, the tears finally came.

Sam stood up from the chair outside Sarah's door and stretched his legs. Hours had passed since Rebecca had left with Jacob. He hadn't heard a sound lately, and the silence made him uneasy. Quietly, he opened the door and peeked inside.

He was surprised to see Sarah out of bed and standing

at the window. Her floor-length robe seemed to swallow up her petite, frail figure. The swish of the door opening drew her attention.

"Hi." Sam stepped into the room. "Are you supposed to be out of bed?"

Sarah offered a feeble smile. "The nurses had me up a few times today. I won't get stronger just lying in bed."

Sam could see she wasn't having an easy time of it. Dark circles colored the skin beneath her eyes in a deep purplish hue. The telltale puffiness told him that she'd been crying. Her sky-blue eyes were clouded over with pain and perhaps even a little fear.

"It is kind of you to show concern, Detective King." Her voice sounded fragile and tired.

"Please, call me Samuel."

He flinched at the sound of his true Amish name slipping from his lips. Donning Amish clothes had returned him to his roots. But the sound of his given name instead of Sam sealed the deal. He had stepped back in time—and it was the last place he wanted to be.

"Samuel." The sound of his name in her soft, feminine voice drew his attention back to her. She smiled again, but it was only a polite gesture. Happiness never lit her eyes. "What can I do for you?"

"I thought I'd poke my head in and make sure you're all right."

"Thank you, but you needn't bother. I'm fine." A shadow crossed her face.

Fine? He didn't think so. Lost in his thoughts, he hadn't noticed the puzzled expression on her face until she questioned him.

"Who are you, Samuel?"

She stood with her back to the window and studied him.

Who was he? He'd told her he was a detective. Was her loss of memory getting worse?

Sarah went right to the point. "You dress like an Amish man. Our men are not detectives." Her eyes squinted as she studied him.

She looked as if she might be holding her breath as she waited for his answer.

"I assure you, Sarah, I am a detective."

"And the Amish clothes? Is it a disguise?"

"Yes—and no. I was raised Amish. I left my home in Ohio and joined the police force about fifteen years ago."

"Ohio? You are very far from home, aren't you?" she asked.

Was that empathy he saw in her eyes? She was feeling sorry for *him*. Didn't that beat all?

"I wanted to get as far away as I could." Sam shrugged, and his mouth twisted into a lopsided grin. "Memories aren't always good."

She pondered his words before she spoke again. "Don't the Amish shun you if you leave?"

He found her words interesting. She could pull the definition of shunning from her memory banks but talked about it as if it wasn't part of her own culture, as if the term was nothing more than something she had read in a dictionary.

"I have no family to shun me."

The gentlest of smiles teased the corner of her lips. "Everyone has a family at one time or another, Samuel."

Her words hit a tender spot. She was getting much too personal. He didn't want to open that door for her. He didn't want to share that pain. He was acting as her bodyguard, nothing more, and the less emotional connection between them the better.

Attempting to change the subject, he said, "I'm sure

you've been up and about enough for one day. Why don't you let me help you get back into bed so you can get some rest."

She allowed him to hold her elbow and support her as she crossed the room. "It must have been difficult for you to leave your Amish religion behind."

Her soft blue eyes stared up at him.

Sam smiled. He was fast learning that she was a stubborn woman, not easily distracted when she wanted to know something, and right now it was obvious that she wanted to know about him.

"I left religion behind, not God," he replied. "I carry God with me every day—in here and in here." He pointed to his head and his heart. "Memories were the only thing I left behind, painful ones."

Since her left arm was useless because of the sling and the IV bag and pole still attached to her right hand, Sam put his hands on both sides of her waist to lift her up onto the bed. Although tiny and petite, he couldn't help but note the slightly thickening waist beneath his touch. The signs of her pregnancy were starting to show, and the protective emotions that surfaced surprised him.

Her saucerlike eyes shimmered with unshed tears, and he fought not to lose himself in their beauty.

"I wish I had some memories," she whispered.

The minty scent of her breath fanned his face, and the slightly parted pose of her lips tempted him to lower his head and steal a taste of their tantalizing softness.

Instead, he removed her slippers and, after she positioned herself back on the pillows, he covered her with a blanket.

"Memories aren't all they're cracked up to be, Sarah. I have memories, but no one to love me. You don't have memories, but you have people who love you very much."

She acknowledged his words with a nod and a pensive expression.

Her fragile beauty spoke to him, stirring emotions and feelings better left dormant. Stepping back, he subtly shook his head and reminded himself of his own rules.

Rule number one: never get emotionally involved with anyone in a case.

Rule number two: remember, at all times, that when working undercover none of it is real. You are living a lie.

"So, you didn't answer me. Why are you dressed like an Amish man, Detective King?"

He searched her face, looking for any signs of fear or weakness. He found instead only interest and curiosity.

"This shooter is highly intelligent. He managed to pull off a massive diamond heist without leaving a trace. No images on surveillance cameras. No witnesses. No mistakes. Until now." He took a deep breath before continuing. "This time he left behind a pouch full of diamonds. The doctors found the pouch pinned inside the waistband of your skirt when you were brought into the emergency room."

He heard her sharp intake of breath, but otherwise she remained still and waited for him to continue.

"This time he was sloppy. He left behind a witness. You." His eyes locked with hers. "He believes that you still have the diamonds in your possession. And he doesn't believe in leaving witnesses behind. There is no question. He will be back."

Fear crept into her eyes. "But you told me the doctors found the diamonds. I don't have them anymore, do I?"

"No. But he doesn't know that."

"Then I have to go away. I have to hide. I can't be around anyone who could be hurt because of me."

His admiration for her rose. She was worried about

people she couldn't remember, and not about the imminent threat to herself.

"The safest thing for you and for everyone else is for you to return to your community. It will be harder for him to reach you and easier for everyone involved to recognize an outsider."

"Is he a threat to anyone besides me?"

"He is a really bad man, Sarah. He will stop at nothing to get what he wants. He could snatch a child. Harm one of your neighbors while looking for information. He is evil in human form." Gently, he tilted her chin up with his index finger and looked into her eyes. "But you and I will work together, and we will not let that happen. I promise."

Sam couldn't believe he had just said what he did.

Promise? The two of them working together? Was he crazy talking to her like this? Like they were a team fighting against evil?

Had he lost his mind?

"How can I help? I seem pretty useless to everyone these days." She smiled but seemed totally unaware of how the gesture lit up her face like a ray of sudden sunshine.

He liked making her smile. He liked easing her pain and stress. He tried to identify this tumble of feelings she stirred within him despite his attempt to stay neutral.

Pity? No. Sarah Lapp was too strong a woman to be pitied.

Admiration. Respect. Yes, that was it. He refused to consider there was anything more.

"I will be moving back to the farm with you," he said. "I'll be your bodyguard while the rest of the police force concentrates on finding this guy. With my Amish background, it makes me the perfect choice for the job. I can blend in better than any of the other officers. I can help maintain respect for the Amish way of life."

"Move in? With me?" Her eyes widened. Her mouth rounded in the shape of a perfect letter *O,* and a pink flush tinged her cheeks.

"We will both be staying with Rebecca and Jacob. We believe you will be the primary target because the shooter still believes you possess the diamonds. You also saw his face and lived. He can't afford to let you talk to the authorities. He will try to make sure that doesn't happen. If we can apprehend him when he makes his move, then everyone else will be safe as well."

"So I am going to be the bait to hook the fish?"

Now it was his turn for heat to rush into his face. He felt embarrassed and ashamed because she was right. He was using her as bait.

"It's all right, Samuel. I understand. I will do this thing if it will help keep the others safe. When do we begin?"

"Soon." He gave her fingers a light squeeze. "You will be in the hospital a little while longer. You still need time to heal. But try not to worry. I will not let anything happen to you while you are in my care."

"I am not in your care, Samuel." Her smile widened. "I am in God's hands."

"Then that is a good thing, *ya?* With God on our side, we can't lose." Sam grinned, hoping his cavalier attitude would build her confidence and help her relax. "Concentrate on regaining your strength. Let me worry about all the bad guys out there."

The door pushed open behind them. Captain Rogers and Sam's partner, Joe Masterson, stood in the doorway. "Detective King, may I see you in the hall for a moment?"

Sam released her hand. "I'll be back. Remember, no worrying allowed. Everything is going to work for good, just the way the Lord intends."

* * *

Sarah tried to still the apprehension that skittered over her nerve endings when she found herself alone in the room. The police were going to use her as bait to catch a killer. Her breath caught in her throat, and she could feel the rapid beating of her heart beneath her hand on her chest. Was she strong enough, brave enough?

You can do this. You must do this. These people need you to help them.

These people? Where had that thought come from? These were her people, weren't they? Her family? She knew she felt a warm affection for both Rebecca and Jacob. They had been wonderfully kind and attentive to her since she'd come out of her coma.

But as much as she hated to admit it, she couldn't feel a connection to them. At least not the kind of connection they seemed to expect. They were kind people. Loving people. But were they *her* people?

She tried again to conjure up a memory, even the slightest wisp of one, of Peter. Rebecca had told her that they'd grown up together and were the best of friends. They were happily married. They were expecting a child.

Sarah placed a hand on her stomach, feeling the slight swell beneath her touch. Their child. And she couldn't even remember Peter's face.

A stab of pain pierced her heart. She must be a shallow person to not remember someone she had obviously loved. Love goes soul deep, doesn't it? Love wouldn't be forgotten so quickly, would it?

Maybe it hadn't been love. Maybe it had been friendship or convenience or companionship. Maybe it was an emotion that hadn't claimed her heart at all. She would never know now.

Her eyes strayed to the hospital room door, and her thoughts turned to Samuel.

She was certain if a person were to fall in love with Samuel, it would be a deep, abiding love. It would be two souls uniting before God. It would last a lifetime and not be forgotten by injury or time.

Her heart fluttered in her chest at just the thought that she might be starting to have feelings for Samuel, before she angrily shooed them away.

Foolish notions. That was one thing she was quickly learning about herself. She was often a victim of foolish notions.

THREE

"There's been another murder."

Apprehension straightened Sam's spine. "Another murder? Who? When?"

"Not here. Follow me." Captain Rogers, Joe and Sam strode briskly to the conference room and took their seats. The tension in the room was almost palpable.

Sam stole a moment to study his superior's face. The past seven days had made their mark. He noted his captain's furrowed brow, the lines of strain etched on each side of his mouth, but what caught his attention the most was the bone-weary fatigue he saw in his eyes. The political pressure to find a quick solution to a complicated, ever-worsening scenario was taking its toll.

The captain folded his hands on the table. "There's no sugarcoating this, so I'm just going to say it. Around 2:00 a.m. last night, Steven Miller was murdered."

"Steven Miller?" Sam leaned back in his chair. "Isn't that the name of the second diamond-heist robber?" He threw a hurried glance at both men. "Didn't we have him in custody?"

"Yep. Same guy." Joe's expression was grim. "We had him under armed guard in a secluded room in a medical center in the Bronx."

"Special Agent Lopez called me first thing this morning." Captain Rogers wiped a hand over his face and leaned back in his chair. "The man was suffocated with one of his own pillows."

"How could something like this happen? He was under armed guard. Did they at least catch the guy?"

"No. He did it on the graveyard shift, when there would be fewer people roaming the halls or in attendance. Once Miller's heart stopped, the monitors went off at the nurse's station. By the time the nurse and crash cart personnel arrived at the room, he had disappeared."

"Any leads? Witnesses?" Sam tried to calm his racing thoughts. This shooter had walked into a hospital and murdered a man in police custody. The degree of difficulty to keep Sarah safe just rose several more notches.

"We believe it was the ring leader of the group," Rogers said. "The same guy we're expecting to show up here. We figure he left here right after the schoolhouse shootings and returned to New York. He spent the week tracking down the whereabouts of his partner in crime, did his surveillance of the medical center and set a plan in motion. He's never left anyone alive who could identify him. He wasn't about to leave one of his team in the hands of the enemy."

"I don't believe this guy." Sam ran his hand through his hair. He could feel his blood throb in a rapid beat on each side of his temple. "You're telling me that he just walked up to a guarded room, slipped inside, killed our witness and left? Why didn't our guards stop him? What did they have to say when they were questioned?"

"Nothing." Joe's expression grew grimmer. "The perp slit the guard's throat. Nobody knows whether it was coming or going, so we're not sure if that's how he gained access or how he covered his tracks when he left. But we think it was on the way out, because a nurse reported that she had stopped and asked the police officer if he'd like a cup of coffee only moments before. She'd just sat down at her desk when the monitor alarm went off."

"What about the surveillance cameras?" The throbbing in Sam's temples became a full-blown headache. He closed his eyes for a second or two and rubbed his fingers on the tender spots beside his eyes before locking his gaze on Rogers. "We're not chasing a shadow. He's a flesh-and-blood man just like the rest of us. Somebody had to see something."

Captain Rogers frowned. "Lopez identified someone he believes is the perp on the tapes. The suspect shows up in multiple camera shots and hides his face every time. Lopez sent the digital images to the FBI labs for further enhancement."

"How did he get into the room in the first place?" Sam shot a glance between his partner and Captain Rogers. "We discussed his security plan with Lopez before he left. It seemed solid."

"It was solid." Rogers sighed heavily. "There was a police presence visible at the elevator banks, both in the lobby and the floor in question. There was an officer at the door of the patient's room as well. Matter of fact, Lopez had created a dummy room with an armed guard, so it wouldn't be easy for someone off the street to easily identify the actual location of our prisoner."

"Yeah, I thought that part of the plan was brilliant myself," Joe said. "I guess the dog we're chasing is smart, too."

"I don't get it." Sam was finding it difficult to process this new information. When he spoke again, he addressed his captain.

"Lopez told me he had a dual checkpoint in place. Every

person entering that room would have had to be cleared—
not just the doctors and nurses, but housekeeping and
dietary would have had to follow the same protocol. They
had to be wearing a photo identification badge, and as
a fail-safe that photo ID had to match the image in the
guard's laptop.

"Even if this guy did manage to create a fake badge,
are you telling me that he was able to hack into the hospital personnel files and upload his picture so he'd pass
the guard's scrutiny?"

A slow, steady burn formed in his gut and spread
through his body. Sam leaned back and threw his arms
in the air. "If the guy is that good, we need him running
the FBI, not running from it."

"He found a loophole," Captain Rogers said.

Sam arched an eyebrow. "Ya think?"

Rogers ignored the sarcasm.

"Lopez set up a failsafe plan for hospital personnel. He
even went one step further and insured that the same police personnel rotated shifts on the door so anyone would
question a stranger in uniform, and the officers would
recognize their replacements. The guard would also log
the time in and out of the room for each visitor."

Sam leaned forward, waiting for more.

"What Lopez didn't consider was that the culprit would
create a fake FBI identity. There wasn't anything on the
laptop for FBI because Lopez intended to be the only one
accessing the room. Unfortunately, he failed to make sure
the guards knew it. That's how we figure he got past the
guard. He pretended to be one of Lopez's own."

"I told you," Joe said. "The guy's smart."

Sam jumped to his feet. "Sarah…"

Captain Rogers waved Sam back down.

"Sit down, King. We're taking care of it."

"We need to move her to another floor ASAP," Sam urged.

"I already talked with her doctor," Joe said. "She's stable enough to be moved out of ICU, so they are making arrangements for a private room as we speak."

"Our men will be handling security on the door—not FBI, not hospital security guards—us." Rogers glared at both of them. "Nothing, absolutely nothing, is going to happen to that woman on our watch. Understood?"

Sam's heart started to beat a normal rhythm for the first time since he'd heard of Steven Miller's murder. He didn't know how this guy could keep slipping through traps, avoiding surveillance cameras and sidestepping witnesses, but it didn't matter. No matter what it took, Sam wasn't going to let the jerk anywhere near Sarah or any of the people who loved her.

With renewed determination, he shoved back from the table and stood. "Captain, with all due respect, don't you think we've talked enough? The ball is in our court now. We'd better get busy setting things in motion. The FBI botched this one, but we can't afford to. If he shows up here, I intend to make sure he's sorry he didn't stay in New York—deadly sorry."

"King." The censoring tone in his superior's voice cemented his feet to the floor. "Your Amish background gives you a leg up over my other officers. I picked you because I believe you can deal with the nuances of this case the best. But for that same reason, you need to be careful. You can't let your emotions color your judgment and jeopardize this case. Everything by the book. Got it?"

Sam nodded.

"Good. Now get back to Sarah. I'm going to finalize the room move with the hospital administrator while Joe coordinates the shift coverage outside her door."

Sam didn't need to be told twice. He was halfway down the hall with the door easing shut behind him before the captain had stopped speaking.

The man made a final adjustment to the fake beard that covered the lower part of his face, being sure to keep his upper lip clean, as was the Amish custom. He stared at the reflection in the full-length mirror on the back of the door and admired his handiwork.

The blond shaggy wig brushed the back of his neck. It made him twitch the way one might with an errant insect racing down your arm, and he shivered with disgust.

He was a man who took great pride in his appearance. His chestnut-brown hair was always faithfully groomed in a short, concise military cut. His fingernails were manicured at all times, his clothing choices impeccable. He'd be glad when this distasteful costume was no longer necessary.

He leaned in for a closer look at the blue contacts he'd worn to conceal his brown eyes. He finished off the look by donning a pair of plain, wire-rimmed glasses. The transformation was amazing.

He glanced down at his outfit. His clothes looked like they'd been woven a century ago. What kind of people willingly dressed like this?

He couldn't wait to get out of this outfit and back into one of his expensive Armani suits. He longed to sit in his butter-soft leather chair, sip the prime Scotch from his private collection and gaze out his plate-glass window overlooking the ocean.

He hooked his fingers behind his suspenders, turned sideways and grunted with satisfaction.

One obstacle still remained.

He glanced at his immaculate nails. He'd have to go

outside and dig in a flower bed. The thought of dirt under his fingernails actually caused his stomach to roil. But these men worked on farms. He imagined they grew used to the feeling of soil and debris as their manicure of the day. The thought made his lips twist into a frown of disgust.

Well, it wouldn't be for long. Diamonds valued in the billions were definitely worth this ridiculous costume and a little dirt, weren't they?

He sighed heavily. He'd have a very limited opportunity to interrogate the woman. But he wasn't worried. If he couldn't get her to tell him where she'd hidden the diamonds before he eliminated her, then he'd find them another way.

He rolled his white sleeves up to his elbows and smiled with satisfaction. Even his own mother wouldn't recognize him. If she had still been alive, that is. He paused for a moment and allowed himself to remember the look of panic and fear he'd seen in her eyes moments before he squeezed the life out of her.

He'd learned many things in his lifetime. One of the most important lessons was that when you needed to infiltrate enemy lines, it was best to blend in, give off an air of confidence, act like you belonged exactly where you were.

It had served him well over the years. His enemies had never sensed his presence—even though he was often right in their midst, hiding in plain sight, as the saying goes.

He stepped back, donned his straw hat and headed to the door.

Nighttime in hospitals always gave Sam the willies. Fewer staff. People speaking in whispers. Tonight his "willies alert" was operating on full throttle. Some cops called it gut instinct. Either way, Sam hated the tension that shot along his nerve endings, the fingers of unease that crept up his spine.

The only discernible sound as he moved through the empty corridors was the soft whirring of machines from open doorways, an occasional whimper of pain or a soft snore.

He was tired. Bone tired. He hadn't had more than two hours of uninterrupted sleep in the past thirty-six hours, and it was beginning to catch up with him. He wasn't a kid anymore—thirty-four on his next birthday, and he needed those eight hours of sleep. Or at least six. Who was he kidding? He'd settle for four if he could snatch them.

He glanced into the rooms as he passed by. They'd taken a risk when they'd moved Sarah to the pediatric floor. He didn't want to imagine the uproar the parents of these children would unleash if they had any idea that the bait to catch a killer had just been moved into their midst.

Captain Rogers had arranged the move. He firmly believed this would be the last floor in the hospital the perpetrator would expect to find Sarah. The captain didn't seem worried about the sensitive location. He was certain that even if the killer did locate Sarah, the children would be safe because they weren't his target. Sarah was.

Sam moved past the rooms filled with sleeping children. He offered a silent prayer that the captain hadn't made a horrendous mistake. As he drew near Sarah's room, he recognized the officer sitting in front of the door.

"Hey, Fitch, how's it going?"

The policeman folded his newspaper and grinned when he saw Sam approach. He gestured with his head toward the door.

"You'd think she was a Hollywood celebrity or something. Orders came down from the top that this is the last day allowed for visitation. It's been a steady stream of Amish folks in and out all afternoon saying their good-byes. First thing tomorrow morning, the only Amish visitor allowed to visit is her former mother-in-law, Rebecca Lapp. No one else. Period."

Sam nodded. "Good. How did everyone else take the news?"

"Truthfully, I think they were a little relieved. They've been taking turns keeping vigil at the hospital all week. I'm sure they want to return to their homes and their farms."

Officer Brian Fitch stood and stretched his back. "I must admit I'm glad they've cut back on visiting. Less work for me. I hear the Amish go down when the sun does, so that's probably why it's been quiet the last few hours." Fitch shot a glance at Sam's Amish attire. "No offense intended or anything."

Sam grinned. "None taken. You're right. The Amish do go to bed early because they are up before dawn each day to begin their chores. Running a farm is not an easy task."

Sam leaned his hand flat against the door and then paused before he pushed it open. "You look beat. Why don't you go stretch your legs? Maybe grab a cup of coffee while you're at it? I'm here, and I'm not going anywhere."

"You sure?"

Sam opened his jacket and patted the gun in his shoulder holster. "I'm still a cop. Remember?"

Fitch grinned. "Yeah, well, you sure could fool me. You look like a natural fit with the rest of those folks. If I hadn't recognized you from our precinct, I'd be checking your ID and trying to talk you out of visiting altogether."

Sam grinned. "That coffee is calling your name, Fitch."

"You want me to bring you something back?"

"No, I'm good."

Taking advantage of Sam's offer to cover the room, the guard nodded and hurried to the elevator banks, not giving Sam a chance to change his mind.

The telltale *ding* of the arriving elevator filled the silence of the night, and Fitch waved. Sam gave him a nod and then entered Sarah's room.

FOUR

The night-light above the hospital bed cast the room in a soft, white haze. Sam looked down upon the sleeping woman, and his breath caught in his throat.

With stress and pain absent from her expression, she looked peaceful, young and surprisingly beautiful.

Long blond hair poked from beneath the bandages that swathed her head and flowed like golden silk over her shoulders. Her cheeks were flushed, giving her smooth complexion a rosy glow. Lost in sleep and probably dreaming, her lips formed a tiny pout. For the second time in as many days, he had to fight the temptation to taste the softness of those lips.

She was young and vulnerable and…

And she took his breath away.

Although he'd found her attractive when they'd first met, he'd been consumed with the business of ensuring her safety and nothing else.

But now…

In the quiet semidarkness of the evening, she reminded him of a sleeping princess and, for one insane moment, he felt an urge to awaken the princess with a kiss.

Shocked by that unexpected and traitorous thought, he

stepped back from the bed as quickly as if he had touched an electrified fence, and then chuckled at his foolishness.

His eyes fell on a white *kapp* resting on the hospital tray table beside Sarah's bed. Rebecca must have placed it there. Sam wondered why. Rebecca had to know that Sarah's injuries would not allow her to wear the *kapp* for quite some time.

Then he glanced around the room and grinned. The middle-aged woman was sly like a fox. This room was a sterile slice of the *Englischer's* world. Monitors. Hospital bed. Even a television hanging on the far wall. This *kapp* resting in plain sight and at arm's length would be a constant reminder of the Amish world waiting for Sarah's return.

He glanced at Sarah's sleeping form one more time before he forced himself to turn away. Before exiting the room, he stepped inside the bathroom. He needed to throw some cold water on his face and try to wake up. His exhaustion was making him think crazy thoughts, have crazy feelings.

He used the facilities and washed his hands. He turned off the water and was drying his hands on a paper towel when a sound caught his attention. He paused and concentrated, listening to the silence.

There it was again. Just the whisper of sound, like the soft rustling of clothing against skin as a person moved about.

He crumpled the paper towel into a ball, tossed it into the trash can and pushed open the bathroom door. It took his eyes a moment to adjust to the change from bright to dim light as he reentered Sarah's room. A tall man dressed in Amish clothing stood in the shadows on the far side of Sarah's bed.

A feeling of unease slithered up Sam's spine. Why

would an Amish man be visiting at this time of night, and without a female companion in tow? Sam slid his jacket aside for easy access to his gun and stepped farther into the room.

"May I help you?" he asked in Pennsylvania Dutch dialect.

The visitor didn't reply. He removed his straw hat and nodded as a person who was apologizing for the late-night visit might. He sidestepped around the bed.

Sam stood too far from the light switch at the door to be able to fully illuminate the room. He had to rely on the soft glow from above Sarah's bed. Because the visitor held the hat higher than normal, Sam was unable to get a clear view of the man's face. His gut instincts slammed into gear. He drew his gun and aimed for the middle of the man's chest.

"Don't move." Sam made no attempt to hide the steel resolve beneath his words. Slowly, he stepped toward the main light switch. He shifted his glance just long enough to see how much farther he had to go.

The visitor immediately took advantage of this momentary distraction, dived sideways and simultaneously threw a pillow at Sam.

Instinctively, Sam raised an arm to protect his face. He pushed the pillow away, recovered quickly from the unexpected gesture and fired his weapon at the man's back as he sprinted out the door. The splintered wood of the door frame told him he'd missed his mark.

Sam sprang forward in pursuit. He'd almost reached the door when his right foot slid out from under him. He struggled to regain his balance and not fall. When he got his footing again, he glanced down and saw a syringe poking out from beneath his foot. He bent down and picked it up.

Suddenly, the monitor beside Sarah's bed erupted in

a loud, continuous alarm. Sam's gaze flew to the screen and horror filled his soul. A flat, solid green line moved across the screen. Sarah's heart was no longer beating.

Before Sam could react, the door burst open. The room flooded with light. A nurse, quickly followed by another, burst into the room and rushed past him to Sarah's bed. While one nurse tended to the monitor and alarms, the other began CPR on Sarah. Seconds later, several other staff members hurried into the room with a crash cart pulled by the doctor close behind.

Sam knew he should be chasing the man who had done this, but his feet wouldn't budge. His eyes flew to Sarah's face. She lay so still, deathly still. He couldn't believe this was happening and, worse, that it had happened on his watch. Feelings of failure were quickly replaced first with fear that he'd lost her, and then by a deep, burning rage that he was helpless once again.

Sam had to leave—now. But he could barely find the inner strength to pull himself away from Sarah's side. This was his fault. But there was nothing he could do for her now. She was in better hands than his, and he refused to let the lowlife who did this escape. Not this time. Not ever again.

Sam pressed his hand on the shoulder of the nearest nurse. When she turned to look at him, he shoved the syringe in her hand. "I found this on the floor. I believe something was injected into her IV."

As soon as she took it from him, he raced for the hospital room door. Before he could pull it open, a woman's scream pierced the air, and the sounds of chaos filled the corridor. Something was terribly wrong. Had the mystery man grabbed a hostage or, worse, hurt one of the children?

Whispering a silent prayer for Sarah, Sam wrenched open the door and darted into the corridor.

A small gathering of people congregated at the end of the hall around the elevator banks. One woman had collapsed on the floor. Sam figured from the shocked expression on her face as he drew near, and from the sobs racking her body, that this was the woman who had screamed. An older gentleman hovered over her and tried to offer comfort.

A man dressed in green scrubs knelt half in and half out of an open elevator. Another man, also dressed in hospital garb, leaned close behind.

Sam pushed his way through the few gathering spectators and up front to survey the scene. For the second time that night, he felt like a mule had kicked him in the gut.

Officer Brian Fitch was sprawled on the elevator floor. One look at his open, sightless eyes and the trail of blood pooling beneath his body said it all. The officer hadn't made it downstairs for coffee.

Sam remembered the sound of the elevator arriving. Their surprise night visitor must have been on it. When the door opened, Fitch was busy nodding to him and must have been caught unaware. One quick, deadly slice across the officer's throat guaranteed that Fitch would never need coffee or exercise again.

Sam pulled out his badge and ordered everyone back, including the hospital staff. There was nothing any of them could do for Fitch now, and he had to protect whatever forensic evidence they'd be able to gather. Sam called hospital security on his cell phone, which he had put on speed dial for the duration of Sarah's hospital stay.

But somebody else had beaten him to it. The second elevator bank hummed to life. He held his hand on his gun and watched two startled guards emerge and stare at the carnage in front of them.

Sam identified himself as an undercover police officer, despite his Amish garb, and flashed his detective's shield and identification. He hoped he hadn't just blown his cover, but at the moment it couldn't be helped.

"Shut down every possible exit," he commanded. "Do it now."

Without hesitation, one of the guards barked orders into his radio while the other attended to crowd control. Sam offered a silent prayer of thanks that if this had to happen, it had happened late in the evening and gawkers were at a minimum.

He hit speed dial on his phone and barked orders the second his partner answered.

"Joe, we have a problem. Get over here, stat."

They'd been partners long enough that when Joe heard the tension in his voice, he was on full alert, and any drowsiness in his tone from interrupted sleep was gone.

"What happened?"

"Fitch is dead. Sarah might be, too. It's total chaos here."

Muttered expletives floated through the receiver. "On my way."

"Notify Rogers and call for backup."

"Okay. Where can I find you?"

"Making sure that every window, door and crack of this hospital is sealed shut so this piece of slime doesn't escape."

Sam ended the call and shoved the phone back in his pocket. He stole one more precious second to glance down the hall at Sarah's door. Every fiber of his being wanted to know what was going on in that room. Had they been able to save her? Or was she dead? The fact that no one had come out of the room yet must be a good sign, right? He had to fight the urge to run back and see what was happening. But no matter what was going on inside that room, he would not be able to help. This time logic won out.

He did what he was trained to do. He compartmentalized his emotions and focused on doing his job. He sprinted down the stairwell, his feet barely touching the stairs, and made it from the fourth floor to the lobby in record time. The sound of approaching sirens and the sight of flashing red-and-blue lights as vehicles slammed to a stop in front of the building told him that both Joe and hospital security had also gone straight to work.

Security guards were already at the entrance. They looked confused and highly nervous, but Sam had to admire how quickly and well they had sprung into action. No one was getting in or out of the building right now except cops.

Sam met with the head of security and asked to see the building's floor plans. Once they were in hand, he began to coordinate a thorough hospital search room by room, floor by floor, while making sure that all exits were covered. For the time being, no one would be allowed to exit, for any reason, from anywhere.

Twenty minutes after he'd called Joe, Sam saw his partner flash his badge and hurry through the front door. He breathed a sigh of relief and stepped forward to greet him.

Joe stopped short when he saw Sam approach. He shoved both hands into his coat pockets and scowled. "Want to tell me what happened?"

"The killer entered Sarah's room dressed in Amish garb." Before Joe could ask, Sam said, "He killed the police officer assigned to guard the door. It was Brian Fitch."

The detectives knew the officer well. A deep frown etched grooves on both sides of Joe's mouth.

"Has anybody notified his wife?"

"Not yet."

"And Sarah?"

"I think the guy injected something into Sarah's IV to stop her heart."

"Is she dead? Were they able to resuscitate her?"

"I don't know. I haven't had a chance to check. I've been organizing the search."

Joe's shocked expression echoed the one Sam was sure he wore as well. "How did this happen? Nobody can be this lucky. The guy's a ghost."

"The guy's no ghost. He's as much flesh and blood as you and me."

"I just don't understand. What happened?" Joe shot a bewildered look at Sam.

"I was there, Joe. Right there." The remorse in his voice was evident. "He got past me anyway and got to Sarah."

"Were you hurt? Did he hit you over the head or something?"

A red-hot flush of shame and embarrassment coated Sam's throat and face. "Sarah was sleeping. I'd stepped into her bathroom to throw some cold water on my face. I didn't hear him come in until it was too late. The room was dark. He threw something at me. It distracted me enough that he was able to get past me."

Joe nodded. "Don't beat yourself up over it. It could have happened to any of us."

"But it didn't. It happened on my watch. Mine, Joe."

Joe grimaced. They'd been partners long enough that Sam knew Joe understood this was about more than what was happening now. This shame and pain and anger stretched back to another time and another place, when Sam had been helpless to save loved ones or bring perps to justice.

Joe patted Sam's arm, empathy evident in his eyes,

and then changed the subject. "Where do we stand with the search?"

"The best I've been able to do is get all the exits covered. We're dealing with graveyard shift. We don't have a lot of warm bodies in the security department right now."

"Where do you want me?"

"Downstairs." Sam walked with Joe to the elevator bank. "I don't believe the guy will try to walk out any of the obvious exits. He's got to know they're the first places we'd shut down. Check every single room in the basement. Housekeeping has storage rooms, supply rooms. I think there are even some employee lockers and break rooms down there. And, of course, the morgue and the autopsy rooms. I've sent security guards to the loading platform by the morgue, but I'll feel better if one of us is checking things out."

"You got it."

The elevator doors opened, and Joe stepped inside.

"Be careful. Fitch was found dead with his throat slashed."

"Great. Just what I want to hear." His mouth twisted in a wry grin just as the doors shut.

Within thirty minutes of the initial alert, the SWAT team, special weapons and tactics, arrived, quickly followed by Captain Rogers. Sam shared what he knew, and they took over command of the ongoing search.

They hadn't located the perpetrator yet. But the hospital looked like a military camp in Afghanistan for all the uniformed and armed personnel swarming the halls. They'd catch him.

Sam threw a glance at his captain and saw the man in a deep conversation with both the SWAT team leader and the head of hospital security. Everything that could be done was being done. Finally, he'd have a moment to find out what had happened to Sarah.

Adrenaline hammered through the intruder's blood stream, and the beat of his heart thundered in his chest. Who knew all those morning jogs along the beach outside his home would have prepared him for the race of his life? He'd made it down five flights of stairs into the basement without anyone seeing him and, he was certain, before anyone could even sound the alarm.

What a rush! He thought it had been too simple when he caught the cop sneaking away for a break. But that's why he loved operating during the graveyard shift. People often snuck away or fell asleep. Made his job so much easier.

But when he'd slipped inside the darkened hospital room, he'd never expected someone might be in the bathroom.

The man had been dressed like an Amish guy, but he wasn't any more Amish than he was. Not carrying that 9 mm Beretta he had fired at him. He was probably an undercover cop.

Undercover cop. Undercover villain. Both disguised in Amish garb. The whole situation was laughable—and dangerous.

He stood with his back against the wall of the storage closet, trying to quiet the sound of his heavy gasps.

He could hear the pounding of feet racing down the corridor and hear the anxious, high-pitched whispers the guards shot to each other as they did a quick search of every room.

The sounds grew louder as the men approached his hiding spot.

He pushed into the far back corner of the room and crouched behind a utility cart with a large white mop and aluminum bucket attached. His hand tightened around the pistol grip of his gun, and he waited.

The door to the closet swung open. One of the security guards scanned the room with a flashlight. Just as quickly, he was gone.

Idiots.

They hadn't even bothered to throw on the light switch or step into the room. No wonder hospital security guards had the reputation of being toy cops. How did they expect to find anyone with such a lazy, half-done search?

He grinned and relaxed his hand, lowering his weapon.

Lucky for them they were stupid, or they'd be dead security guards just about now.

He stepped out from behind the cart when a sudden flash of light made him squint and raise his hand to his eyes. Someone had thrown on the switch, illuminating the room, and it took his eyes a second to adjust.

"Don't move! Drop your weapon and slide it over to me. Do it now!"

This wasn't a security guard. He looked into eyes of cold, hard steel. This must be a detective. A smart one, too.

Slowly, he lowered his weapon to the floor and kicked it in the detective's direction.

The detective moved farther into the room, never lowering his gun. He stepped to the side and withdrew a pair of handcuffs with his free hand. "Nice and easy now. Put your hands out where I can see them, and slowly walk over here."

Again, he did as requested.

The detective clasped a cuff onto his right wrist.

With speed resulting from years of martial arts training, he spun, released the blade sheathed on the inside of his sleeve and slashed the detective's throat.

The killer grinned. He always loved the look of surprise and horror on his victims' faces, and this detective looked shocked, indeed.

He removed his Amish clothes and quickly donned the detective's cheap brown suit. His lips twisted in disgust. The pants were about two inches too short, the waist at least two sizes too big, and the sleeves of the suit jacket revealed too much forearm. He shoved some towels under his shirt and cinched his belt tight to hold them in and his pants up.

He glowered at the pant length. When a scenario like this played out in the movies, the exchanged clothes were always a perfect fit. Just his luck this wasn't a movie. But he'd have to make do.

He slipped the detective's badge onto his belt, retrieved both guns from the floor and took one last look around to make sure he left nothing of significance behind. His eyes paused on the dead body.

"Sorry, buddy. You were good. Much better than those security guard wannabes. But I'm better. You never stood a chance."

He used a towel to wipe away fingerprints on the light switch and doorknob. He shut off the light, glanced up and down the empty corridor, stepped into the hall and leisurely walked away.

FIVE

Sam couldn't breathe.

He tried. But only shallow wisps of breath escaped his lips.

As soon as he could move...or react...or feel anything but pain, he'd remind himself to inhale deeply.

Yep. He'd do that. Just as soon as the world stopped spinning.

"Do you recognize this man?" A male nurse kneeling beside the body on the floor glanced up at him. "Is he one of yours?"

Tears burned Sam's eyes. His throat clenched, making it impossible for him to speak. The nonchalance of the strangers doing their jobs roiled his stomach. To them, this was just another body. To him...

Sam glanced at the body of the man, dressed only in underwear, lying on the utility room floor. He hated what his eyes relayed to his brain, but he couldn't seem to turn away.

How did this happen? Dear God, why?

"Hey, are you all right, buddy? You look pretty gray in the face. You're not getting sick on me, are you? You're a cop. You see dead bodies all the time, don't ya?"

"Bert, give him a minute." The female nurse gently

touched Sam's forearm. "You know this man, don't you, detective? He's one of yours."

One of yours.

Sam nodded.

Yes, he was one of his. His partner. His best friend. His only family. And now he was dead.

"His name is Detective Joseph Masterson. He was my partner."

"I'm so sorry." Her eyes supported the truth of her words. "Is there anything we can do to help?"

Sam took a deep breath and steadied himself. Rational thought returned, and his inner cop took command.

"I need both of you to step away from the body and try not to touch anything else on the way out of the room. This is a crime scene now. Please wait in the hall for a few minutes until I can get your names and contact information." He ushered them out of the room and grabbed the closest officer in the hallway. "Who discovered the body?"

The cop pointed to two women waiting at the end of the corridor. "Guard this door," Sam said. "No one comes in—absolutely no one—until our forensic team arrives. Make sure to take contact information from these nurses while I speak to the women at the end of the hall."

The cop nodded and did as requested.

Sam approached the women and flashed his detective shield. "My name is Detective King. I'd like to ask you a few questions." He glanced at their name tags. The younger female was a nurse. The matronly woman's tag identified her as custodial staff. "Ms. Blake," he spoke to the nurse. "I'm told you're the one who called us."

"That's right." She seemed perplexed at his Amish garb, but accepted the badge at face value.

"Did you find the body?"

The body.

He couldn't believe he was able to treat this like any ordinary crime scene when, internally, he was reeling in pain.

Dear Lord, continue to give me the strength I need to do my job and get through this night. First Sarah. Now Joe. Help me. Please.

"She found the body." Ms. Blake nodded to an older woman sitting beside her. "This is Mrs. Henshaw. She went into the room to get supplies, and then I heard her scream...."

Sam arched a brow and studied the drawn features of the elderly woman. It was evident that the shock of her discovery had taken its toll, and he knew he needed to tread lightly. "Thank you for speaking with me, Mrs. Henshaw. I'm sure you want to get home. I'll try to keep my questions short and to the point."

The woman looked up at him, her eyes glazed and distant.

"How long ago did you discover the body?"

She glanced at her watch. "I'm not sure. Thirty minutes, maybe."

Mrs. Blake nodded. "At least. Maybe a bit longer. We checked the body for vitals before I made the call."

"Do you remember touching anything in the room?" Sam asked.

"No. When I saw his throat had been cut, I knew he was dead, but I checked his carotid for a pulse anyway. Then I pulled out my cell and called it in."

Sam took a deep breath and fought to keep the images she relayed out of his mind.

"Do either of you remember seeing anything or anyone suspicious? Anything out of the ordinary?"

Both women shook their heads.

"Do you remember passing anyone in the hall?"

"Policemen," Mrs. Henshaw said. "There were security guards and police officers running up and down the halls. I wasn't sure what was going on. I waited for the halls to clear before going to get my supplies." A moment passed, and her face crunched in concentration. "There was something…"

Tension tightened Sam's body as he waited for her to continue.

"I didn't think much about it at the time but…" The woman looked directly at him. "I did see a man. He came down the hall after everyone else had already gone."

Sam honed in on her words. "Did he do or say anything?"

"No."

"What caught your attention? Why do you remember this particular individual?"

"Well, he was walking kind of slow, like he was taking a leisurely stroll in the park, and I guess I noticed that because everyone else had raced past."

"Anything else, Mrs. Henshaw?"

She frowned. "Yes. His pants. They didn't fit. They were about two inches too short."

The shooter had changed into Joe's suit.

"Thank you both. If I have any more questions, how can I reach you?" He pulled a small pad out of the inside pocket of his jacket.

Both women gave him their contact information.

"King!"

Sam glanced over his shoulder, then thanked the women for their help and joined the captain. It took only a few minutes to bring his superior up to speed.

The captain wiped a hand over his face and sighed heavily. "I'm sorry, Sam. Losing a good man is never easy for any of us. Worse if it's your partner."

Sam nodded. "Any word, Captain? Has anyone caught him?"

"Not yet. Unfortunately, we suspect he has already slipped past us." The captain nodded toward the utility room. "Everyone's been looking for a man in Amish garb. I've got a BOLO out now on him using Joe's suit, badge and gun as a description."

"That sounds like a plan. Be on the lookout for a detective when every detective and cop on the force is part of the search. Don't want to bet on the success of that one." Sam couldn't hide the bitterness and sarcasm in this voice. "We've got to get this creep. If it's the last thing I ever do…"

The captain clamped a hand on his shoulder. "I've got this one covered. Go home, son. Get some rest."

"I need to call Cindy." The last thing he wanted to do was have to tell his partner's wife that her husband wasn't coming home. His distaste for the assignment must have been evident in his eyes, because the captain slapped his shoulder a second time.

"It's been handled. I sent a squad car and a couple of our most empathetic men over to her place. Didn't want to take a chance she'd hear it from another source. Now get some rest. Go see her after you've gotten some sleep."

"Thanks, Captain."

Sam pushed open the stairwell door and sprinted up the steps. No way was he going home. Not until he found out what had happened to Sarah.

When he entered the fourth floor, the first thing he noted was the absence of guards in front of Sarah's room. His mind raced with a variety of scenarios on why no one would be posted there, but the only one that made sense was the one thought he refused to believe. Sam's feet felt as if they were encased in cement, each step forward harder than the one before.

He paused outside the room, threw his shoulders back and then pushed the door open.

A black mattress, empty and stripped of its sheets, waited silently for its next occupant.

The air gushed out of Sam's lungs.

Where was Sarah? Was she...

His mind couldn't even complete the thought.

He blinked hard and continued to stare at the empty bed. She couldn't be dead. A sense of failure, mixed with a multitude of other emotions, washed over him.

Oh God, please...

Sam was glad God could read hearts, because at the moment he was totally incapable of completing the prayer.

"May I help you?"

Startled, he spun toward the voice. The nurse's expression registered suspicion, even a tinge of fear, as she stood in the doorway, poised to run if necessary.

"Can you tell me what happened to Sarah?"

The nurse eyed him skeptically. Of course she'd be wary. The entire hospital was in shutdown mode. They'd been told the killer had been dressed in Amish clothes— and here he stood in Amish clothes. The staff had also been told the killer had stolen a detective's badge and gun, so showing his identification probably wouldn't help this frightened nurse feel any better.

"Are you family?" she asked.

Not up to explanations, Sam simply nodded.

The nurse pushed the door wider, but made sure not to enter the room and kept in plain view of people in the hall. Smart lady.

"Sir, I'm sure Dr. Clark will be happy to speak with

you. Take the elevator to the seventh floor and ask for him at the nurse's station."

"Can you at least tell me if Sarah is alive?" Sam heard the hopeful tone in his voice and realized this case was quickly becoming more personal than he had intended it to be.

"Please, sir. The doctor will answer your..."

Sam sidled past her and bounded toward the elevator before she had a chance to finish her statement. He tapped his foot impatiently and watched the numbers light from floor to floor. A sense of anticipation filled his senses as he got off the elevator and skidded to a stop at the nurse's desk.

"I'm looking for Sarah Lapp."

Don't say she's in the morgue. Please don't.

The nurse looked up from her paperwork. "I'm sorry, sir. Mrs. Lapp is not allowed visitors."

She's alive. Thank you, God.

A tsunami wave of relief washed over him. Now if he could just get this nurse to give him the information he needed. He pasted on his best smile and tried again. "You don't understand—"

"Sam."

He turned his head at the sound of his name. Dr. Clark approached, stretched out his hand and grasped his in a firm handshake.

"Sarah made it? She's going to be okay?" Sam asked, not paying any attention to Dr. Clark's quizzical expression at the emotion evident in his voice.

Dr. Clark ushered Sam away from the nurse's desk and asked him to walk with him. As they moved down the corridor, Sam could see a uniformed guard sitting in front of one of the ICU rooms.

"Sarah's going to be fine. Thanks to you. The vial you

gave the nurse held the remnants of potassium chloride. A large enough dose can stop a heart. We were able to act quickly and bring her back."

"Will she be all right?"

The doctor nodded. "She's going to be fine." He raised his eyes. "Someone up there must be looking out for her. I can't believe everything this woman has survived over the past two weeks. Unbelievable."

Sam frowned. He felt awkward asking, but he needed to know. "The baby?"

"As far as we can tell, the baby is as strong as the mother. All is well."

It felt like one of those old-fashioned leaded vests had just been lifted off his chest. His lips twisted into a smile for the first time that day.

"Thanks, Doc."

"You're welcome. Please tell me that you apprehended the man who committed these horrible crimes." Worry creased the doctor's forehead into two deep, parallel furrows.

"Not yet."

Dr. Clark's frown deepened. "The best thing we can do for all concerned is to make other arrangements for Mrs. Lapp. Under the circumstances, the hospital cannot accept responsibility for her safety...or the safety of our other patients."

Sam nodded.

Dr. Clark continued, "I believe that with some medical precautions put in place, moving to a safe house or, perhaps, to a more familiar environment will help with her recovery. Her stress level here is off the charts. Understandably, of course."

They walked the last few feet to her door, but stood outside to finish their conversation. Sam recognized the officer on duty, acknowledged him and turned his attention back to the doctor. "How quickly can we move her?"

"I want to keep her under observation for another twenty-four hours. Barring any unforeseen complications, she will be released then."

"Does the captain know?"

"Not yet. I haven't seen him since the hospital shut down."

"I'll fill him in. We'll start making arrangements on our end. Is Sarah awake? I have a few questions."

"Yes, she's awake. Her mother-in-law is with her. But please keep your visit short and try not to upset her. She needs her rest."

Sam nodded, and the doctor walked away.

Sarah's alive. She's going to be okay and so is her child.

Despite the nightmare this evening had become, he couldn't help but smile as he pushed open the door and stepped into the room. He was going to see Sarah.

SIX

Sarah caught movement in her peripheral vision, turned her head and smiled. "Detective King."

"Samuel." He gestured at his clothing. "It won't do me any good to dress like this if you announce me as an undercover cop every time I walk into a room."

A giggle escaped her lips, seeming to surprise them both. "You're right. Sorry, Samuel."

Sam respectfully inclined his head toward the older woman and acknowledged her presence.

"Do you have any information for us?" Rebecca's face wore lines of concern. "Have they found the man who did this terrible thing to our Sarah?"

"I'm sorry—not yet. But I'm sure we'll hear something soon. The hospital has been shut down. Every floor and room is being searched as we speak."

Rebecca seemed satisfied with Samuel's reply. "My husband went home at dinnertime. I was sleeping in one of those reclining chairs in the family waiting room when Dr. Clark sent a nurse to tell me what had happened." She squeezed Sarah's hand, and tears glistened in her eyes. "God is *gut,* Sarah. He has returned you to us twice, *ya?*"

Sam leaned a hand on the bed rail. "I hate to have to do this now, but I need to ask you a few questions."

"It is all right, Samuel. Do what you need to do." Sarah looked up at him and waited.

"Do you remember anything that happened this evening? You were asleep when I first entered the room. Did you wake up at any time?"

Sarah offered a weak smile. "Of this, I remember, Samuel." She locked her gaze with his. "I had been sleeping, but I started to wake up when you came into the room. I was—what's the word?—groggy? My eyes didn't want to open, but I knew you were there." Her smile widened. "When I did coax them open, I saw your back as you walked into the bathroom. I closed my eyes again. I think I started to drift back to sleep. I know this is not helping you."

"You're doing fine."

Her heart skipped a beat and fluttered like a symphony of dancing butterflies in her chest when he smiled at her. Before she could ponder the strange feelings she seemed to experience in this man's presence, he encouraged her to continue her story.

"The man must have entered the room as soon as I stepped out. Did you see him?"

"Yes."

Samuel's eyes widened, and she sensed his anticipation and tension.

"Can you describe him?"

She chewed on her bottom lip as she tried to bring the memory of the man's face into her mind. "I…I'm not sure. The light in the room was dim. I had been sleeping."

"Do your best, child." Rebecca patted her hand. "Anything you can tell Samuel will help him."

Sarah broke eye contact with both of them and stared at the ceiling as she tried to remember every detail she could. "He had blond hair and a yellow beard that reached the top of his chest. He was dressed in Amish clothes. He looked...ordinary."

"Did you recognize him, Sarah? Was he one of the men at the school?" Rebecca asked.

"I don't remember anything that happened at the school."

"Still nothing?" Rebecca asked. "No one?"

Sarah knew the woman kept hoping that she would someday remember her son, Peter. But today wasn't that day.

She couldn't bear to see the disappointment in Rebecca's eyes or the anticipation in Samuel's. She squeezed her eyes shut and tried as hard as she could to remember something, anything. When she opened them again, she looked from one to the other and knew she had nothing to offer. Sadness almost overwhelmed her.

"I'm so sorry. I can't help you."

"What happened when he approached your bed?" Sam tried to prod her memory. "Did he say anything to you? Think, Sarah. It might be important."

"Yes. I remember that he did speak to me. I knew from his words that this was the man who had killed my husband and who had shot me."

Rebecca gasped. Her hand flew to her chest, but she remained silent.

"Take your time, Sarah. No one can hurt you now. Try to remember what he said." Sam's calm, warm voice encouraged her.

"He asked me what I did with the diamonds. He said he knew I had the pouch." An increasing anxiety caused her voice to tremble. "I told him I knew nothing about his diamonds." Fear slithered up her spine at the memory. "His eyes were so dark, so cold and...and evil."

Sam reached out and clasped her hand. "Go on. You're doing fine. What else did he say?"

Sarah found Sam's touch strangely comforting, and the way her body trembled with fear, she needed all the comfort she could find.

"He grinned at me," she said. "I remember thinking how perfect his teeth were. Really white and straight and clean. His breath…I remember a cloying, minty scent when he leaned close…almost too minty…my stomach turned. He leaned close to my ear and whispered, 'I will find where you hid those diamonds. I don't need you to do it.'"

Her heart galloped inside her chest, but this time it was fear that caused the pace. "That's when I saw him pull something out of his pocket. He held it against the tube attached to my arm. My chest became tight, like something very heavy was sitting on me. I couldn't draw a breath. That's all I remember." A tear slid down her cheek. "I woke up in this room with Rebecca by my side. She told me what had happened. That is all I know."

"She has answered your questions. You must leave her now," Rebecca insisted. "She needs to rest."

Sam nodded and released Sarah's hand. He stared into those mesmerizing blue eyes. "Thank you."

"I have been of no help."

"That is not true. You have helped quite a bit. Thanks to you, we know that he will stop at nothing to find the diamonds. He was bold enough to walk into enemy camp and risk being recognized as an intruder. In New York, he dressed as an FBI agent, and here, as an Amish man. So our belief that he would return has been proved correct."

Sam sighed heavily. "You have also proved our theory that he would not leave behind any survivors. He tried to kill you. He did kill the one member of his team we had in custody in New York. He also killed the guard who had been sitting outside your door." The darkened intensity in his eyes told her that he had more to say, and it was very difficult for him. "He also killed my partner." His voice broke as he tried to conceal his grief.

Rebecca gasped. "Detective Masterson has been killed?"

Sarah looked into Sam's eyes and thought her heart would break when she saw nothing but pain staring back at her.

"I am so sorry, Samuel."

He hung his head in silence.

"You said the man guarding my room was also killed?"

Sam nodded and didn't seem to be able to meet her eyes. When he did look at her, he reminded her of a little boy in pain who needed cuddling and comfort, but this brief glimpse of vulnerability didn't last more than an instant before the hard-edged detective reappeared.

"I apologize. I let my guard down. It almost cost you your life. It did cost the life of a good officer, as well as the life of my partner."

"This was not your doing, Samuel. You must not blame yourself." Sarah knew from his reaction that her words held little comfort.

"I was standing in the room with you. Just feet away, and I let him slip by. I promise I will not let anything like that happen again."

"God willing."

Both of them glanced at Rebecca after she spoke.

"God is in control, Samuel, *ya?* He will decide what does or does not happen." Her steady, unflinching gaze caught his.

Sam straightened his shoulders. The tone of his voice was harsher than normal when he replied. "Sometimes

God needs a little help to bring the bad guys to justice, Rebecca. That's my job, and that's what I intend to do."

"Justice, Samuel? Or vengeance?"

Sam bristled beneath the censure. "Call it what you want. If I hadn't been there this evening, if I hadn't stepped out of the bathroom when I did, Sarah wouldn't be with us right now."

Rebecca shot a loving glance Sarah's way. "It was God's will that Sarah remain with us. He may have used your presence, Samuel, and for that I am most grateful."

Ashamed of himself for lashing out at the woman, he lowered his head and apologized. "I'm sorry I spoke harshly. You're right. God uses many things to bring about His will in this world…and many people."

Rebecca smiled at him and nodded.

The door opened. Sarah thought Captain Rogers looked even more exhausted than Samuel, if that were possible.

"What are you doing here?" he growled in Sam's direction. "I thought I told you to go home and get some sleep."

"I will. I had a few loose ends that I needed to tie up first, sir."

The captain glowered, but refrained from any further admonishment.

"Have you found the man who did this terrible thing?" Rebecca asked.

The captain's face wore the strains of exhaustion. "No. I'm sorry. He got away."

"But how?" Sarah asked. "There were so many of you looking for him."

Captain Rogers sighed heavily. "He killed one of my detectives and switched clothing with him. When we initially started our search, my men were told to look for someone in Amish garb. They weren't looking for one of their own. By the time we got the word out about the wardrobe change, we believe he had already escaped."

"We are so sorry to hear about the death of your men, Captain." Rebecca folded her hands. "They lost their lives trying to protect us. We will remember them and pray for their families."

Sarah shot a glance at Sam and was again moved by the pain she saw in his eyes. The loss of his partner cut deeper than he was willing to admit.

"Thank you, ma'am," Captain Rogers replied.

"Do you think he is gone for good?" Sarah asked. "No man would be foolish enough to come back again when the whole police force is looking for him, would he?"

"That is exactly what he is going to do, Sarah." The captain's steely gaze and no-nonsense voice held her attention. "He plans on killing you, the teacher and the children who were in that classroom. We've suspected that from the beginning. His actions in the past two days have confirmed it."

Sarah's stomach twisted into a tight, painful knot. The anger and determination she saw in both men's eyes upset her. She didn't need past memory to recognize the tension and fear in the room now.

She was willing to accept God's will for her life, and she trusted Him to protect her. But her throat constricted when she thought about the children. She knew in her heart that God would protect them, too. But she had looked into the stranger's face. Pure evil had stared back.

A chill shivered down her spine when she thought of the stranger's threats.

She glanced at Samuel, and a sense of peace calmed her.

Maybe Samuel was right. Maybe God used people to

help carry out His will, and He could be using Samuel. She certainly hoped so. She would pray about it.

"What happens now?" Rebecca asked, swinging her gaze around to everyone in the room.

"Dr. Clark will be releasing Sarah tomorrow," Sam said.

Captain Rogers looked surprised. "So soon?"

"Yes, he told me just a few moments ago. He feels Sarah will be safer somewhere else. And, of course, the administration is screaming about liability."

"I'll need time to get the wheels in motion." Rogers looked at Rebecca. "Can we count on your help, Mrs. Lapp? Will Sarah be going home with you? Are you still willing to let Detective King accompany you?"

"Of course we will be taking Sarah home." Rebecca moved closer to the bed and busied her hands, gently tucking the blanket around Sarah's body as a mother might when tucking in a child for the night. When she finished, she looked at the two men.

"As for Samuel, my husband has already given his permission, and Jacob is a man of his word. Nothing that has happened here tonight will change that." She sent a kind, warm glance Sam's way. "Besides, Samuel has had a great loss of his own. Losing a partner must be a difficult thing, *ya?* Like losing a member of your family? It will be good for Samuel to be in a quiet place where he can reflect and pray and feel the tender mercy of God's healing touch."

He cleared his throat. "Okay, then. Let's get this thing started. We have twenty-four hours to make it happen."

"No. We have sixteen hours," Captain Rogers corrected. "Both of us need sleep. I don't want to see your face for at least eight hours. That's an order."

Sam nodded. "Understood, Captain. I'll be here first thing in the morning to take Sarah home."

Home.

A place she couldn't remember, but just the word made her long to get there. She tried hard to conjure up a mental image. What did the house look like? Did they have a barn? Horses? Cattle? Were they farmers tending fields of grain, or did their fields contain rows of corn? With all that had happened, would the Amish community still gather for celebration and praise? Or would the death of the bishop's son change everything?

Once Sarah saw the house and the farm, would it help refresh her memory? She held current memories of many faces that had come to visit her during this ordeal. They had claimed to be her friends. Would she be able to rekindle those relationships once she returned home? She hoped so. Maybe she wouldn't feel so lost and alone anymore.

In twenty-four hours, she would know the answer to all the questions tumbling around in her head. Somehow the thought of returning to a place where she had once forged roots, a place where she had once belonged to a community and a family, was strangely comforting…and oh so terrifying.

SEVEN

Sarah glanced down at her clothing. Gone was the print hospital gown. She wore a black apron that covered a good portion of the light blue dress beneath it. The dress draped her body loosely, fell slightly below her knees and brushed against her black opaque stockings. She smoothed her hand across the material.

Because of the many visitors she had had over the past week, Sarah knew this was typical Amish garb. So why didn't it feel familiar? Why couldn't she picture in her mind another time and place where she might have been dressed this way?

"Is something wrong?" Rebecca's heavily lined face wore a quizzical expression. "Are you feeling ill? Is this task too difficult for you right now?" Before Sarah could reply, Rebecca hurried forward. "Here, let me help you with your shoes."

"Thank you, but I can put on my shoes." But when Sarah bent down for the shoes, her head spun, and pain seized the left side of her temple.

Rebecca leaned over and retrieved the shoes. "You are not yet fully recovered. You are going to need some help with things you used to do for yourself. Do not let pride make you stumble before the Lord."

Sarah accepted the chiding with a respectful nod. But was it pride? Or a fierce determination to get better as quickly as possible and regain her independence?

A knock on the door drew their attention.

Sarah's heartbeat skipped when Samuel poked his head inside. She hadn't seen him for more than a moment or two since yesterday. He'd been making arrangements for her safety after she left the hospital. She'd missed him— and that thought surprised and unsettled her.

Samuel nodded a polite greeting to Rebecca as he entered, and then froze. The intensity of his gaze as his eyes roamed over her Amish clothing made her self-conscious. She smoothed her apron and wondered if some piece of clothing looked silly or out of place.

Rebecca coughed, breaking Samuel out of his reverie.

"Forgive me," he said. "I apologize for staring." He smiled at Sarah. "It is a surprise to see you out of hospital gowns. You look—" he seemed to search for the proper word "—healthy." His smile widened. "You look like you're ready to get out of here and go home."

Sarah smiled in return. "That I am."

Dr. Clark had told her that familiar surroundings might help her regain some of her memory. Sarah was counting on it with an anticipation so intense she found it almost hard to breathe.

"Are you ladies ready?"

"Almost." Rebecca slipped the white *kapp* that had been lying on the nightstand on top of Sarah's bandages. It was a tight squeeze, but she got it placed properly. She tilted Sarah's face up. "We are ready now, *ya?*"

Sarah squeezed Rebecca's hand. She had grown fond of the woman, grateful that she came every day regardless of how difficult it must be for her. It didn't take black clothes to show that Rebecca was grieving. All someone had to do was look at the pain and fatigue evident in her eyes, body language and facial expressions. Yet still she came, every day, and sat beside her and told her stories of the farm, and occasionally stories of the life she'd shared with Peter.

Sarah learned they had not only known each other since childhood but had been good friends, which was a bit unusual in the Amish community, since boys and girls often had separate activities and chores. But Sarah had been a bit of a tomboy as a child. She loved to climb trees and play baseball and fish. Rebecca's eyes would light up when she'd tell Sarah tales of her escapades—the catfish she'd caught that weighed more than any of the boys' and the tale of her broken arm when she'd been spying on the boys swimming and had fallen out of the large oak tree on the back of their property by the pond.

"You always pushed boundaries. I had to practically tie you down when it came time to teach you how to cook and sew." Rebecca actually smiled for the very first time since this nightmare began.

"Why didn't my mother teach me those things? Why did it fall on your shoulders?"

A dark cloud passed over Rebecca's expression, but she quickly recovered. "That is another conversation for another day, *ya?* Right now I think it is best to get home."

Sarah held her tongue, but she couldn't help wondering why Rebecca seemed reluctant to talk about her mother. Was there some dark secret no one had told her about? And if Rebecca was hiding behind secrets, how could she be sure that what she told her about Peter and their marriage was the truth?

Before Sarah could question the older woman more, a nurse entered the room pushing a wheelchair. "These are your discharge instructions. Your medications are listed.

So are signs and symptoms that you should report immediately to Dr. Clark if they occur."

Sam took the papers from the nurse's hand. "Thank you. We will go over these with a fine-tooth comb once we get home." He folded them and tucked them inside his jacket. "Sarah won't be needing the wheelchair. You can take it out with you."

"It's hospital policy that every patient is wheeled safely to the curb," the nurse insisted.

"Her safety is exactly the reason we can't afford to have her leave in a wheelchair." Sam shifted his attention to Sarah. "I was afraid the news media would catch hold of this story. After the hospital lockdown and the two murders, they have. National news crews have been camped outside all night, hoping for a picture for the tabloids or a few quotes for their papers. They've been trying to locate your room and slip in to see you. You wouldn't believe how creative and sneaky some of them have been. Hospital security has had their hands full. If we push you outside in a wheelchair, they'll descend on us like vultures."

"So what must we do?" Rebecca twisted her hands together and looked at Sam with concern on her face. "Sarah is not strong enough for such attention."

Sam looked at Sarah with a steady gaze. "Are you strong enough to walk out of here if I help you?"

Her stomach flipped under his scrutiny. When he looked at her like that, she wanted to please him. She just wasn't sure she could. "I think so but…" She lowered her voice and her eyes. "I'm willing to try, but I'm not sure I can."

"That's my girl. I knew I could count on you to give it a try. Don't worry. I'll be with you every step of the way."

My girl? Had he just said that to her?

He turned to Rebecca. "Do you have any extra Amish clothes with you? Perhaps a *kapp,* and possibly a shawl?"

"Yes," Rebecca replied. "I have some extra clothes with me. I have been sleeping in one of those fancy chairs that tilt back. Jacob brought me a bag from home so I could change and freshen up in the public bathrooms."

"Good." Sam grinned at the nurse. "I think you will look lovely in a white *kapp,* don't you?"

The nurse stammered and sputtered a weak protest as she realized he intended to put *her* in the wheelchair. She glanced at the two Amish women. Their faces were pale with fright and concern. She looked back at Sam and smiled. "Why not? I love pranks. This should be fun. Maybe I'll even make it on national TV."

Sam gently cupped Sarah's elbow, and the heat of his touch sent waves of tingles through her body. When he spoke, his voice was warm and tender. "How do you feel? Are you able to do this?" His eyes locked with hers, and she thought she'd drown in their darkness. "Am I asking too much of you? If you can't do the walking, we will use the wheelchair. We'll try to camouflage your exit."

Her pulse beat like war drums against the soft tissue of her wrist. She wasn't sure if it was the result of her anxiety about evading the press and going home, or whether it was a reaction to the strong, masculine presence of the man standing beside her. The man who had been kind and supportive and…and almost irresistibly attractive from the moment she'd opened her eyes.

"How far must we go?"

"Not far. We'll take the elevator to the basement and slip out the morgue entrance. I will be with you every step of the way."

Rebecca clasped Sarah's other arm. "So will I, child.

God will be with us too." Rebecca handed a *kapp* and shawl to the nurse. "I hope these will help."

Sam asked an officer to push the disguised nurse in the wheelchair through the front entrance while they headed toward the elevators.

Just as the three of them were about to make their exit, the door opened again.

"Jacob." Rebecca looked at her husband in surprise. "What has happened? Why are you here?"

"You are my wife. Sarah is my daughter-in-law. You need me. Where else would I be?"

Although there was no physical contact between them, there was a sense of intimacy. They obviously loved each other and it showed…in the kindness of their words…in the gaze of their eyes…in the gentleness of their voices. Sarah couldn't help but wonder if this was what her relationship with their son, Peter, had been like.

A deep sadness flowed over her that she felt no feelings for Peter. Neither good nor bad. She couldn't even draw his image into her memory. The Amish did not approve of pictures, so Rebecca was unable to show her a wedding photo or any other.

Sarah glanced at Samuel. There was kindness and gentleness and something else with this man. She felt more fondness for this stranger than she did for the man who had been her husband. It wasn't the way it was supposed to be, not the way she wanted it to be. And it troubled her greatly.

Almost as if he could read her mind, Sam seemed to assess both the change in the atmosphere of the room and its possible reason. Instantly, he took charge.

"Come." He spoke with authority. "We have to slip out before the press realizes that isn't Sarah we sent out front."

Without a word, they hurried from the room. They rode

the elevator in silence. Sam exited first, checked that the corridor was empty then summoned them to follow.

Sarah knew he shortened his steps to keep pace with hers. She moved as quickly as she could down the long, empty corridor, but her rubbery legs had no strength. She feared they would crumple beneath her at any moment. Her heart beat in her chest like a runaway horse, and for the first time in many days, fear threatened to claim her composure.

Sam had arranged for a driver to be waiting for them at the morgue loading dock. The four exited the building and crossed the dock with synchronized movements to the steps to the parking lot.

Beads of sweat broke out on Sarah's forehead. She felt as if the blood had drained from her face, leaving her light-headed and dizzy. Her chest hurt, and suddenly it became difficult to breathe.

"Wait! Please." She began dragging her feet. "I can't…I can't breathe." Her hand flew to her chest, and she gulped for air.

Jacob and Rebecca had reached the car, and they turned to see what delayed them. Sam gestured them on. "It's okay. Get in the car. We'll be there in a second."

Sam faced Sarah. He clasped both her forearms in his hands and locked his gaze with hers. "Sarah?"

"I don't know what's wrong. My chest…it hurts…and I…I can't breathe."

"Listen to me. You're having a panic attack. Dr. Clark warned me that you might, once you left the hospital and the stress hit you." He locked his gaze with hers, the intensity of his stare mesmerizing her. "I'm not going to let anything happen to you." He drew her closer, almost as if he could transfer his strength to her. "You can do this. But you have to trust me."

"There they are! On the loading dock!"

Sam and Sarah looked in the direction of the voices. Two women, each holding a microphone in hand, raced toward them. A couple of men carrying cameras sprinted behind the women.

"We have to get out of here," Sam said.

Sarah's legs trembled as if they were made of gelatin instead of flesh and bone. "I can't." Certain her legs would no longer support her weight, she leaned heavily against his chest. "I'm sorry, Samuel."

Without hesitation, he scooped her off her feet.

She could feel his muscled strength supporting her legs and back as he carried her to the car. She clenched his shirt, its softness rubbing against her cheek. The clean scent of fresh linen mingled with the appealing, warm scent of his skin as she clung to him, and for a crazy moment in time she had no desire to release her grasp.

By the time they'd reached the first step, her heartbeat had slowed and her breathing returned to normal. Raising her eyes to meet Samuel's, Sarah knew that everything would be okay. God would protect her...and He would use Samuel to do it. Peace and gratitude replaced the terror that had been flowing through her veins just moments before. She smiled up at the man who held her in his arms.

"Take me home, Samuel. Please, I just want to go home."

EIGHT

It was early evening when they arrived at the house. Looming in the shadows of twilight, the two-story white clapboard house looked much like many of the others they'd passed along the way. A large red barn loomed to the left. They passed a multitude of fenced areas. In the distance, two horses grazed in the meadow.

Once the driver stopped the car, Jacob got out and hurried ahead to ready the house. Sam came around and helped both Rebecca and Sarah out of the vehicle.

Sarah stood for a second and looked around the property. She breathed in the heavy smells of fertile earth, manure and animals common to a working farm. She climbed the steps to the front porch, all the while trying to retrieve memories of times past, but none came.

Jacob met them just inside the door. Several kerosene lamps bathed the home in a warm, soft glow. "It is *gut* to have you home, Sarah." He helped Rebecca take off her coat and then helped Sarah with hers.

"I will make us some hot tea." Rebecca crossed to the propane-powered stove and put the kettle on.

Sarah glanced around the living room. She noted a sofa, several chairs and scattered tables, but the focal point of the room was an impressive stone fireplace.

"Please, sit. Rest." Jacob gestured toward the kitchen table. "I have to bring in my horses. I will be back shortly."

"Do you need help?" Sam offered.

"*Danki,* no. Sit. Rest. It was a long trip, and I believe you have gotten little sleep in the past weeks."

Rebecca placed hot tea and a plate of fresh, homemade cookies in the middle of the table.

The scent of chamomile and chocolate chips teased Sarah's nostrils and made her realize she had barely touched her dinner.

"There's nothing better to ward off a night's chill than a hot cup of tea and a sweet treat. Come, both of you. Sit. Eat," Rebecca said.

"*Danki,*" Sam answered in the Pennsylvania Dutch dialect, his tone light and friendly. He bit into a cookie. "*Gut.* Did you know the *Englisch* have a saying that the way to a man's heart is through his stomach? These cookies are probably what prompted the saying."

A smile teased the corner of Sarah's mouth when she saw the blush of pleasure stain Rebecca's cheeks. What do you know? She wasn't the only one to succumb to this man's charm.

Rebecca, mindful of Sarah's arm in a sling and her frail health, poured her a cup of tea and placed two cookies on a small plate in front of her.

The three of them sat in companionable silence, enjoying the quiet and the treat, comfortable enough with each other not to feel obligated to fill the silence with idle conversation.

Sarah felt at home amidst the simple, plain surroundings, even though she had no concrete memories of ever being here before. But it only took a glance outside, now that twilight had ebbed to darkness, to remind her that until this man was caught, she would have no safe haven.

The back door opened, and Rebecca waved her husband inside.

"Come, Jacob. Sit. The tea grows cold."

Jacob took a seat and grinned. "I'm coming, *lieb*. I already know the secret that I am sure Samuel has just discovered. A bite of your cookies on a person's lips is a moment of pure joy."

Rebecca's blush deepened, and she placed an extra cookie in front of her husband.

Sarah grinned. Cookies might bring joy to the men, but for her, it was witnessing the strong and loving bond between the two people who were turning out to be the only family she had.

Sam and Jacob kept the conversation at the table flowing. They discussed hopes for the fall's harvest, the farmer's market prices, the plans for next year's planting.

Sarah smothered a yawn with her hand, and immediately Rebecca rose from the table. "You must be exhausted after today's journey, child." She picked up one of the oil lamps. "Come, I will show you your room."

Sam stood, clasped Sarah's elbow and helped her to her feet. His touch sent a surge of energy through her body, leaving tingles and confusion in its wake.

"Rebecca is right." Sam gently trailed a finger down her cheek. "You need your rest."

His eyes darkened with an intensity Sarah didn't understand. As they gazed into each other's eyes, there was an intimate pull between them, almost as though they were the only two people in the world.

More confused and disconcerted about the feelings that were growing for this man, Sarah broke eye contact and took a step away.

They were right. She was more than tired. She was exhausted, weak and disheartened. She'd expected a flood of memories to burst forth once she'd seen the farm, and she could barely hide her bitter disappointment when it did not happen.

Sarah followed close behind Rebecca, her path illuminated by the oil lamp Rebecca had given her. Rebecca paused outside a door to the right of the stairs, opened it and stood aside, looking hopeful and expectant.

Sarah recognized Rebecca's expectation. She was hoping that once Sarah entered the bedroom, her memory would return. She couldn't fault the woman; she longed for the same thing and dreaded that it wouldn't happen.

She stepped inside. The oil lamp bathed the room in a soft glow. She noted the pretty patchwork quilt on the double bed, the plain curtains at the two windows, the rocking chair beside a sturdy table that held a Bible.

Sarah's eyes missed nothing, and her heart grew heavy. She released the breath she'd been holding. Nothing. No memories. No feelings. No past. She could barely turn to face Rebecca.

The older woman forced a smile to her face, hurried to the chest against the wall, pulled out a clean, fresh, cream-colored floor-length flannel gown and laid it out on the bed. "Will you need me to help you dress?" Rebecca glanced at Sarah's sling.

"No. I'll be fine."

Rebecca nodded. "This should keep you warm, but if you find the gown and quilt are not enough, please come and tell me. The nights this time of year can sometimes chill a person to their bones." She crossed to the door. "If you need anything, child, anything at all, our room is only three doors down on the right."

"Danki." Sarah answered in the Pennsylvania Dutch dialect, but she wasn't sure if it was something she was pulling from her memory or something she'd heard so

many times over the past few weeks that it felt natural saying it.

After Rebecca left, she placed the oil lamp on the nightstand. It was a struggle to get out of her clothes and don the flannel gown, but she managed. Sitting on the edge of the bed, she glanced around the shadowed room. That's how her mind felt—a mixture of clear images, shadows and darkness. Would she ever remember her former life?

It was frustrating not to remember anything of her childhood, her teens, her adulthood. Questions swirled through her mind.

What kind of person was she? Was she kind and loving, or did she have a selfish streak? Was she hardworking or lazy? Had she laughed easily, loved deeply, or was she more withdrawn and quiet?

Everyone in this small community knew the answers to her questions. Why couldn't she find those answers within herself?

A tear slid down her cheek. She felt so afraid and alone.

But she wasn't alone, was she? The thought brought her comfort, and she began to pray.

In the bright light of morning, Sarah took the opportunity to study her surroundings. The room was clean, neat and simple. A plain wooden oak chest stood against a far wall. Small oval rag rugs rested on each side of the bed to warm one's feet against the chill of the wooden floor. Two hooks hung on the wall next to a small closet. Were they to hold the next day's clothing? Or perhaps a man's hat? Peter's?

The thought reminded Sarah that in the not too distant past, she'd shared this room with someone. Someone she'd been told she loved. She spread her hands over the slight swell of her belly. That love had created this new life.

Even if she had no mental images of Peter, she was certain she'd have a clearer picture of the man when this child was born. She would only have to look at the child's eyes, or the color of hair, or the tiny baby smile, and she would be able to "see" her husband. If nothing else, she was certain that at that moment she would feel love for the man who had given her such a precious gift. But would she ever remember Peter himself, and the life they'd shared?

Dr. Clark had warned her not to expect too much of herself, that memories would come gradually, if they came at all, and not to stress over it.

Easier said than done.

Sarah couldn't deny that she'd had huge expectations when she'd come home. As foolish as it might seem now, she'd believed that once she actually saw her home, her memory would return. Disappointment left a bitter taste in her mouth and her heart heavy. But she wouldn't let it color the day. She would be grateful that she was home and healing.

Sarah followed the rich, mouthwatering aroma of coffee and freshly baked bread downstairs to the kitchen. "Good morning, Rebecca."

The woman spun around from the sink. "*Guder mariye.* Did you sleep well?"

"Yes, *danki.* The trip home must have tired me more than I thought. I fell asleep as soon as my head hit the pillow."

"Did sleeping in your own bed help you remember anything?"

Rebecca's expression held such hope, and Sarah's inability to give the woman the answers she longed for filled her with guilt and sorrow.

"I didn't remember anything. I didn't even dream last night." When she saw the light in Rebecca's eyes dim, pain seized her heart. "I'm so sorry. I know you were hoping for more from me."

"The only thing I am expecting from you, child, is for you to do your best to regain your health. Nothing more. You will remember in God's time if He desires it." Her brow furrowed. "Should you be out of bed? I was fixing a tray to bring to your room."

"I was just about to ask that same question."

Sarah didn't have to turn around to know that Samuel stood behind her. He filled every room he entered with a strong, masculine presence. Besides, she would recognize the deep, warm tones of his voice anywhere.

The polite thing to do would be to acknowledge him and answer his question. She glanced over her shoulder to do just that, but the smile froze on her face and her breath caught in her throat. He stood closer than she'd expected. Close enough that she should have been able to feel his breath on the back of her neck.

Mere inches separated her from the rock-solid wall of his chest. She couldn't help but remember how warm and safe and protected it had felt to be held in those muscled arms, cradled against that chest.

She took a step back and stumbled awkwardly over her own feet. Sam's hand shot out to steady her. "See, it is too soon. You should be in bed." Concern shone from his eyes and etched lines in his face.

"I'm fine." She eased her arm out of his grasp. "I tripped over my own feet. I don't know if I was an awkward oaf in my old life, but it looks like I am now." She grinned. "And yes, I should be out of bed. I've been in bed for two weeks. I may not remember much about my old self, but this new self, this person I am now, can't stand being cooped up for one more minute."

Rebecca chuckled behind her. "That's not a new self,

Sarah. That's who you've always been. A dervish of activity from sunup to sundown, even as a little one." Rebecca patted her hand on the table. "Come. Both of you. Sit down. Eat."

"I can't remember the last time I sat down to a meal that didn't come out of a hospital vending machine. I'm starving." Sam beat Sarah to the table and pulled out a chair for her before he sat down.

Rebecca laughed. "Good. I like to feed people with healthy appetites." She carried a heavy, cast-iron skillet to the table and filled his plate with potatoes and sausage. Scrambled eggs were already in a bowl on the table. She set out a second small plate filled with slices of warm bread and a Mason jar of homemade strawberry jam.

"Yum." Sam's stomach chose that moment to growl loudly, and both women laughed.

Sarah watched every movement he made while pretending not to notice anything at all. She noted how long and lean his fingers were when he lifted a slice of bread. She smiled to herself when she saw the tiniest bead of jam at the corner of his mouth.

A warm flush tinged her cheeks when she realized how happy she was when he was around, and then she grew confused and unhappy with herself for that same reason. Should she be allowing anything, even friendship, to develop with this man? He was an *Englischer.* She was Amish, or at least that's what everyone told her she was. She wished she felt Amish, or English, or anything from anywhere—if she could only own the memory.

One thing she did know for sure. She was an assignment to Samuel, and he would be leaving as soon as his assignment was over. Didn't she have enough chaos in her life without adding unreturned feelings to it?

She stole another glance at him. She couldn't help but

admire his strong, chiseled features, the square chin, the pronounced cheekbones, the angular planes and the deep, dark, intense eyes that seemed to be able to look at a person and see into their soul.

Was she gravitating toward him because, besides Rebecca, he had been the only constant in her life for the past two weeks whom she could rely on in an otherwise frightening, blank world of strangers and fear?

Or was the reason simply a woman being drawn to an attractive, kind man?

Either way she had to learn to dismiss these new feelings in an effort to discover the old ones. She had to concentrate on remembering the past and forget the temptation of daring to think about a future. There was no future for Samuel and her. There never would be.

"Where is Jacob?" Sam smeared jam on a second slice of warm bread. "I'd like to ask him if there is anything close to the house that I might help him with today. Maybe muck the stalls in the barn?"

"Jacob is mending a fence in the back pasture," Rebecca replied. "He left at first light. I am expecting him back anytime now."

No sooner had the words had left her lips than the back door opened and Jacob strode into the room. He hung his coat and hat on the hooks by the door, slid out of his boots and padded in his socks to the table.

Rebecca slid a mug of hot coffee in front of his chair before he even sat down.

"*Guder mariye,* everyone. The skies are clear. The air is sweet. Looks like a good day for working in the fields." Jacob rubbed his hands together in anticipation and took a slice of bread from the basket.

"What can I do to help?" Sam asked. "I know work is never truly done on a farm, but I am limited in how far I can wander from the house. I was hoping you might have something for me in the barn. I can muck stalls, feed animals. I also saw carpentry equipment."

"*Ya,* that was Peter's work. He built cabinets and furniture. He was working on a new table and chairs to present to Josiah and Anna. They are to be married this month."

"Aren't weddings held in November, after the harvest?" Sam asked.

"*Ya,* but this is a special occasion. Josiah has a *gut* job opportunity with an Amish family in Ohio. Peter finished the chairs he was making for them, but not the table." Jacob's eyes dimmed. "I will have to find time in my schedule to finish it for him."

"Let me."

Jacob cocked an eyebrow. "You know woodworking?"

Sam shrugged. "I am better working in the fields, but my father taught me to sand and stain and varnish. I need to be close to the house to protect Sarah, but it doesn't mean I can't share in the work."

Jacob nodded, and a new respect crossed his expression. "That is *gut. Danki,* Samuel. I will accept your help with the table."

Sam glanced out the kitchen window. He tensed and rose to his feet. "A buggy passed by the window," he said in answer to the questioning looks on everyone's faces.

Pounding on the front door drew their attention.

Jacob rose to answer it, but before he could the door opened like a burst of wind had pushed it, and Benjamin Miller stormed into the house. He strode to the kitchen doorway, his demeanor angry.

"Forgive me, Jacob, for entering without your permission, but the matter is urgent."

Jacob's tone of voice was low and calm but stern as he faced his friend. "What could be so urgent, Benjamin, that you could not wait for me to open the door? You have frightened my wife and Sarah."

Sam remained standing. Sarah thought he looked like a panther poised to strike, his hand subtly hidden within the folds of his jacket. He must be wearing a gun. The thought made shivers of apprehension race up and down her arms. She did not like guns, and she did not want to be reminded that Sam was as comfortable wearing one as he was his pants or boots.

Benjamin removed his hat. "I apologize." He pointed an accusing finger at Sam. "But I told you that allowing this man into our homes would only bring trouble to us, and now it has."

"What are you talking about? What trouble?" Jacob asked.

"There is a man in town. He is going business to business asking where he can find Sarah—and the man protecting her."

NINE

"*Kumm*, sit." Jacob gestured to a vacant chair at the table. "Rebecca will pour you a cup of *kaffe*, and you can tell us what you know."

Benjamin glared at Sam as he stepped past him. After he took a sip of his coffee, he leaned in toward Jacob as if he was the only person in the room to hear.

"I was at the hardware store when Josiah came in and told me. The whole town is in a dither. No one knows what to do or say."

"What are folks saying?" Sam tried not to appear annoyed when Benjamin directed the answer to Jacob as if he was the one who had asked.

"We cannot lie. Everyone has simply said that we cannot help him."

"Did you see this man?" Jacob asked.

"*Ya*, he came into the hardware store just a few minutes after Josiah. He was of average height and dressed in an *Englisch* suit and tie. He had bushy, bright red hair and wore wire-framed glasses."

"Did you hear what he said to the store clerk?" Sam asked. "Did he have an accent? Any distinguishable features like a scar or mole on his face?"

Still ignoring him, Benjamin finished his coffee and

then spoke to Jacob. "He pulled out some kind of wallet and flashed the badge inside. He said he was a police detective."

"But that is a lie." Jacob glanced between Sam and Sarah, who had paled like the milk in the glass in front of her. "If he truly was a police detective, he would know where Sarah lives, and he would know Detective King."

"*Ya,* he is lying. Everyone knows it. He brings trouble to our town." For the first time since sitting at the table, Benjamin made eye contact with Sam. "He is following you. You should not have come here."

"Benjamin, please tell us what else the man said." Rebecca refilled his coffee cup.

"He told the store clerk that the woman he was searching for, Sarah Lapp, had been kidnapped from the hospital by the man who was claiming to protect her. He asked if anyone could tell him what farm or family she belongs to, or if they'd seen her in town."

Sam ignored the accusatory glare directed his way. "Could he have been a newspaper reporter? They have been known to use less than truthful tactics to get a story."

Benjamin shrugged. "The town is full of reporters. They travel in packs like wolves. They carry cameras and climb in and out of big motor vans. They wear their pictures on a badge on their clothes."

"So what do we do?" Rebecca held fingers to her chin, and concern filled her eyes. "We cannot let this man near our Sarah."

"I don't intend to let that happen, Rebecca. Don't worry," Sam assured her.

"Maybe I should leave this place." Sarah joined the conversation for the first time. Her eyes were earnest, her tone anxious. "If I go away and hide someplace else, maybe the man will follow me. Maybe it will keep the *kinner* safe."

"The children will not be safe, Sarah, no matter what you do. It is not beneath him to use them to flush you out, even if you did hide someplace else. It is better for you to stay here. It will be easier to protect you."

"Is there anything we can do to help?" Jacob asked.

"Yes. Talk to everyone you know. Ask them to keep their silence. Tell them it is not only Sarah's safety they will be protecting, but also the children's."

Sarah stood. Her legs wobbled beneath her, and she held on to the table edge for support. "I cannot let this man hurt the *kinner.*"

Sam hurried to her side and supported her right arm with his hand. "The only thing I want you to do right now, Sarah Lapp, is to rest. You must get stronger if you expect your memories of that day to return. If they return, that is when you will be the most help."

"Samuel is right, child." Rebecca took Sam's place at Sarah's side. "You've had enough excitement for now. Let me help you back to bed. You haven't been out of the hospital an entire day yet."

Sarah looked at each man at the table, and then fixed her gaze on Sam. "What happens now, Samuel?"

"We wait."

"That's it? Just sit and wait for a madman to come and hurt our *kinner,* or kill me, or both?"

Benjamin jumped to his feet and shouted. "You must go! Maybe if you go, he will leave and we can all go back to our lives."

Benjamin flailed his arms in anger, but Samuel saw beneath it and recognized the fear. He kept his voice calm and his tone reassuring.

"Tell me, Benjamin. If a wolf stalks a man's sheep, will the wolf go away because the shepherd decides to leave the flock and go home?"

Sam paused while he waited for the other man to consider the wisdom of his words. When Sam spoke again, his voice, though calm, held a note of steel.

"This man will come for Sarah…and when he does, I will stop him."

Sarah thanked the good Lord that the day had ended much quieter than it had started. She gently rocked back and forth on the front porch and watched the sun set over the newly planted fields. Despite the disturbing news at breakfast, once the discussion had ended, the men had gone about their chores, and the day had passed peacefully.

Samuel had kept busy in the barn with the table he had promised Jacob he would finish. Although he rarely left the barn, Sarah could feel his eyes upon her whenever she stepped out of the house. At first it was unsettling and made her uncomfortable, but after she'd had some time to think and pray about it, she realized his intention was to keep her safe, and she was grateful.

Rebecca crossed the porch and sat down beside her. "Let me help with the string beans."

Sarah laughed. "Please, I may not be able to use my left shoulder, but my hand works. I can break string beans into smaller pieces for dinner."

Rebecca glanced into the bowl resting on Sarah's lap. "And it is a good job you do."

Once Rebecca had settled into a soft, rhythmic rocking beside her, Sarah dared to broach the subject that had been weighing heavily on her mind all day.

"Rebecca, tell me about my family. In the hospital you changed the conversation when I mentioned my mother. No one has claimed me as daughter or sister or aunt. Do

I have a family? Beside you and Jacob…and Peter, of course."

A shadow crossed Rebecca's face, and her rocking quickened.

"I do not wish to cause you any grief," Sarah continued. "But of course, you must understand how difficult it has been for me not to know who I am, who I come from. I am afraid those memories may not return, and you…you could help me with some of the answers to this darkness inside."

Rebecca dropped her head and remained silent.

"Was I an evil person? Did I come from a bad family? Is that why talking about it is difficult for you?"

Rebecca's eyes widened, and her mouth opened in a perfect circle. "Lord, help us. Where would you get a notion such as that?"

"Because the question brings you pain. I assume it is bad memories I am asking you to recall."

"Nothing could be further from the truth, child. The pain I feel is that of loss and grief for all the wonderful people who were part of my life and are now home with the Lord."

Rebecca reached over and patted Sarah's knee. "Your grandmother and I grew up together. We were best friends. Her name was Anna. She married when she was still in her teens and had a daughter soon after, a beautiful girl named Elizabeth.

"Elizabeth was a dervish of energy, a tornado of sunshine and light…just like you were, child. Elizabeth met an *Englisch* boy and left our community to marry him and live in his world. It broke Anna's heart but…" Rebecca shrugged. "She understood this thing called love."

"When your father was killed in a factory accident,

Elizabeth brought you home. You were about five at the time. Such joy! Such happiness you brought to Anna's eyes every time she looked at you." A cloud passed over Rebecca's expression. "And when your mother took ill and died, you were the only thing that kept Anna's heart from shattering into a million pieces."

Rebecca smiled at her. "Your grandmother died just before your tenth birthday. Jacob and I brought you into our home and raised you like one of our own. We were overcome with joy when you married Peter and became a true daughter, not just one of my heart."

Rebecca's eyes glistened with tears, pain, grief—and something else, something she found harder to identify. "You are all Jacob and I have left now. We have lost Anna and Elizabeth and…and Peter…" The catch in her words gave her pause.

"I'm so sorry. I didn't mean to cause you pain."

"Ack. Sometimes life is painful, child. That is what makes it life and not heaven." She smiled broadly. "But it is not all pain. We still have you, *lieb*. And the child you carry is God's blessing to all of us. He knows how painful it has been for me. Not to see my son's smiling face or hear his voice or watch him hammer away on the furniture he crafts in the barn. Part of my heart shattered that day in the school house. But not all of it…"

She cupped Sarah's chin in her hand. "God made sure He left me with enough of a heart so I could fill it with love for you and for my grandchild. He took Peter to be with Him. That was His will, and sometimes it is hard to understand His ways. But He left a little part of Peter with us. For that, I am so very grateful. God is *gut*."

Rebecca stood. "*Kumm.* It will be dark soon. The men will be tired and hungry. I am sure there is something I can find for you to help me with despite your sling. It will be like old times, fixing dinner together for our family."

The two women embraced and then walked together into the house.

Later that evening, Sam saw Sarah standing on the porch. She stared up at the night sky and seemed to be studying the stars.

"For a person who just got out of the hospital, I find you spend most of your time outside." Sam's boots scraped loudly against the wooden floor of the porch.

Sarah turned her head and tossed a smile his way. The light from the kerosene lamp danced softly across her features.

"I've been cooped up much too long. I like to feel fresh air on my skin." She turned her eyes back to the sky. "Have you ever really looked at the sky, Samuel? God is an artist, and He uses the sky as His palette. I watch in awe as the patterns and colors change from dawn to dusk to the inky blackness of night. Even then, He decorates the darkness with stars to light our way and to give us hope."

Sam stepped behind her and wrapped a quilt around her shoulders. "If you insist on living on the porch, you must start wearing a jacket or sweater. The days are pleasant, but the temperatures still dip in the mornings and evenings. You're going to be a mother. You must keep yourself warm and healthy."

Almost on cue, a rush of cool air brushed past them and he could feel her quiver beneath his touch. She pulled the quilt tighter and burrowed into its warmth.

"You have looked at the sky for hours, Sarah. Even God has gone to bed," he teased her.

Sarah chuckled. "True, I suppose. I find it easier to think when I'm out here."

Sam gestured to a rocker. "I have been standing all day. I would like to sit now, and I can't if I am supposed to be protecting you. How about protecting me for a little while? Sit with me so I can give my legs a rest."

She did as requested. "I think it would be your eyes that need rest, Samuel. They bounced in my direction and then back to your chores so often, I'm surprised you can still see straight."

He laughed hard and deep, the booming sound breaking through the silence of the night. No words needed to be spoken as they rocked together in perfect unison.

"You are right, Sarah," Sam said. "You created quite a dilemma for me. A bodyguard cannot guard a body if he is not watching it, and a man cannot be a man if he stays in another man's home and does not attempt to pull his own weight. So my poor eyes got a workout for sure." He rested his left ankle on his right knee.

"How is the table coming along? I saw how hard you worked. You went over every inch, your movements steady, your attention to detail evident."

"Tomorrow I will do the final touches and it will be ready." He reached over and squeezed her hand. "Maybe you will take pity on my eyes and sit with me in the barn."

"Breathe in fresh air on the porch, or inhale the smell of hay, manure, animals and varnish in the barn? Sit in shadows when I can be outside and feel the warmth of the sun on my face. Hmm?" She held an index finger to her lips as if seriously considering the proposition. "Sorry, I think not, Samuel. You will just have to finish your chores faster and come sit in the sunshine with me."

"I do sit in the sunshine whenever I am with you."

The unexpected compliment seemed to surprise them both. A heavy silence fell over them. The only sound on the porch was the rhythmic swishing of the rockers. When Sam spoke again, his tone was thoughtful and serious.

"Talk to me, Sarah. What deep thoughts trouble you so much that you stare into the horizon for hours searching for answers? I know the past two weeks have been difficult. I understand. I am just wondering if there is something more…something deeper that troubles you."

A tear slid down her cheek, and she hurried to wipe it away.

"You can talk to me, you know. Listening is part of bodyguard duties and comes absolutely free of charge."

In the soft glow of the kerosene lamp, Sarah saw warmth and empathy in his eyes. She knew she could feel safe baring her soul to this man because he was a stranger. She didn't have to choose her words with care for fear of saying the wrong thing or having something she said cause pain, like it sometimes did when she talked with Rebecca or Jacob. She felt she could talk to him about anything—except the unsettling feelings and questions she had about him, of course.

He reached out and clasped her hand. "Talk to me. I can be a good listener."

She inhaled deeply. Maybe it would be helpful to talk with someone who might be able to understand the disappointment and fear gnawing inside. Grateful for an open ear, she kept her voice low so as not to disturb Rebecca or Jacob inside.

"I thought coming home would end all my troubles. I thought when I saw the house, when I returned to familiar surroundings and slipped back into a normal daily routine, that everything would be okay."

Silence hung in the darkness between them.

"I expected my memory to return. Expected answers to the thousands of questions I have inside."

"I take it you haven't had any flashes of memory?"

She shook her head, oblivious as to whether he could see the movement in the dim light.

"Dr. Clark warned you, Sarah. He said your memories would probably come back slowly, maybe in flashes, and you should be patient. He also told you that they may not come back at all."

"I know." Her voice was a mere whisper on the wind.

"Can you live with that? Can you cope with the fact that your memories may never return?"

The warmth of his voice flowed over her, filled with concern and offering her waves of comfort, but still she felt lost and defeated. "I'm not sure. I don't know how it will be if this is a permanent situation. The only thing holding me together right now is hope…hope that it will all come back, that I will remember again."

"And if you don't?"

The silence became heavy and oppressive, stealing her breath, causing her fingers to tremble and her toes to nervously tap against the wooden floor.

"Calm down, Sarah. You're starting to have another panic attack. Take a couple of deep breaths. It will be all right."

He stopped rocking, pulled his chair around to face her and moved in closer so she could see his face in the dim light.

"You're scared."

She nodded.

"What frightens you the most?"

She thought for a moment, and then locked her gaze with his. "I'm scared to death that I will never know who I am, who I was…" She nodded with her head toward the house. "Who they expect me to be." She lowered her eyes. "They are good people. They have been hurt enough. What if I can't be the person they want me to be?"

A burst of anger raged through her. "Why did this happen? What am I supposed to do with all this emptiness?" She jumped to her feet, held on to the porch rail and stared out into the night.

"Do you have any idea what it feels like to be me?" she asked. "I can't remember the people around me, the same people who shower me with love and gaze at me with such high hopes and expectations." She sighed deeply. "I can't even remember *me*.

"I am told I was an *Englisch* child who was raised by an Amish grandmother and then adopted by the Lapps after her death. But what does that make me? Am I *Englisch* because I was born in your world? Or am I Amish because I was raised as a child in this one? I can't remember anything about either world, so how can I answer that question?

"I am told I was a dervish of energy. Is that why I want to be busy all the time? Why I long to be outside and moving? Or is it fear and restlessness from thoughts I cannot bear that drive me?"

She paced, and Sam didn't speak or try to stop her.

"Do I like strawberry jam? Scrambled eggs? Sausage? Can I cook? Can I sew? Do I have friends? Do I care about anybody? Am I a person who should be cared about?"

Sarah's fears shone through her eyes.

"I was married to a man I can't remember. There isn't even a picture I can look at so I can try to remember his face. Married, Samuel. Partners in life, in love. I can't remember any of it. Does Peter deserve to be forgotten? What kind of person does that make me?"

Her voice rose. She could hear the frustration and anxiety in it, but she couldn't control it.

"I'm pregnant. I'm carrying a precious gift, a blessing. But what kind of mother will I be? How will I teach this child the ways of the world when I can't remember ever taking the path myself? How can this child grow to love me? How can *anyone* love me when I don't know me well enough to love myself?" Her voice rose an octave. "I have to remember. Everyone needs me to remember. I don't know what I will do if I can't."

Sarah had to physically fight the urge to dart away, to flee into the darkness and try to outrun the fear.

Sam stood and gathered her into his arms. She nestled firmly against the warmth of his chest. The sound of his voice rumbled against her ear. She could feel the gentle breeze of his breath through her hair with each word of comfort.

The words he spoke were not important. They were comfort words. It was the strength of his embrace, the solid wall of his presence that soothed her. He offered her a safe haven to air her fears without judgment. He offered her friendship and empathy. Sarah may not be able to prevent disappointing the people who knew her in the past, but Samuel wasn't a part of her past. He knew her only as she was now. She truly believed that God had sent him into her life to help her when she needed it most… and that thought brought her peace.

"I'm sorry." She eased out of his embrace.

She didn't have a chance to finish the sentence before he cupped her chin with his hand and forced her eyes to lock with his.

"You have nothing to apologize for, Sarah. You are as much a victim in all of this as anyone. Remember that."

He brushed his fingers lightly against the path of tears

on her cheek. "You can sit and wallow and feel sorry for yourself. You have the right to do that." He smiled down at her. "Or you can look at this as God's gift…an opportunity to be anyone you want to be."

She arched an eyebrow.

"You tell me you don't know if you were a good person or bad, selfish or kind? Okay, so choose. It doesn't matter who or what you were. None of us can change one moment of the past, no matter how much we might want to. But God has given you the present and it is a gift, isn't it? Decide what kind of person you want to be. Will you be loving and kind to others? Will you be hardworking and helpful? Your choice, isn't it?"

He smiled down on her. "You will be a wonderful mother because you care for your child so much, and he or she isn't even here yet. Think about it, Sarah. You can take the journey with your child. The two of you can learn to play in the sunshine. You can both decide together whether you like the taste of turnips or prefer the taste of corn. You can read books together each night before bed. You might find that you enjoy them just as much as the child because you will be reading them for the first time.

"Who cares if you can cook? If you can't, you can learn. Who cares if you can sew? Try it. If you can remember the stitches, *wunderbaar*. If not, it is only another lesson to learn. You can start your life over again, Sarah. Many people I know wish they could have that chance."

The truth of his words washed over her, and she felt a new resolve, maybe even a little happiness blossom within. She chewed on her bottom lip. "But what of Jacob and Rebecca? What if I can't be the person they remember?"

He slipped his arms around her waist and drew her close again.

"They loved the person you were. Now they will love the person you will grow to be."

She smiled and allowed herself to burrow against him one more time. She closed her eyes. He felt so warm and comforting and safe.

Suddenly his body tensed. She raised her head and searched his face.

"What?"

He didn't speak but stared hard into the darkness. The tension in his body made his formerly comforting hands tighten to steel. His grasp almost hurt as she eased out of his hold.

She turned her head and followed his gaze. A tiny ball of light shone in the distance. She squinted and tried to focus to get a better look. As she stared harder across the dark, empty fields, the light grew larger, brighter.

"Samuel, what is it?"

His features were stone-cold, his expression grim.

"Fire."

TEN

"Fire? Are you sure?" Sarah grasped the porch post and stared hard at the horizon. What had begun as a tiny glimmer was now an ominous orange light that grew in height and width even as they watched.

The sharp clanging of a bell broke the silence of the spring night. Seconds later Sam's cell phone rang, the musical notes clashing with the continued clang of the farm triangle. He mumbled a few words in reply to whatever he was hearing, shoved the phone back in his coat pocket and raced for the barn.

"Samuel?"

"Stay there. Don't move!" he yelled over his shoulder as he ran.

Sarah watched in alarm as the light became a looming two-story-high monster of flame on the horizon.

Jacob and Rebecca raced onto the porch.

"What's happening?" Jacob stumbled toward Sarah in a half hop as he bent down to pull one of his boots on. Rebecca, tying the sash of her robe over her long flannel nightgown, was close on his heels.

Before Sarah could respond, Jacob yelled, "That's Benjamin's place! There's a fire!" He turned and clasped his

wife's forearms. "I must go. I'll be back as soon as I can."
He kissed her on the forehead.

Rebecca nodded. "God speed and keep you safe."

Just as Jacob moved to the steps, Sam ran out of the
barn, pulling one of the horses behind him. He brought it
to a stop at the base of the stairs. "I thought it would be
faster to saddle the horse than hitch the buggy."

"Danki," Jacob replied, throwing his foot in a stirrup
and mounting up. The horse, sensing the tension and probably smelling the smoke, pawed the ground and tried to
rear, but Jacob took control of the reins and had the steed
settled and listening to commands in no time. "Take care
of the women."

Sam nodded and watched Jacob gallop away. He
climbed the steps and joined the women. They watched
in silence as what had been a glimmer of brightness now
filled an uncomfortable stretch on the horizon, with ominous fingers of light that seemed to touch the sky.

"Let us say a prayer." Rebecca clasped their hands.
They bowed their heads and prayed for safety of all who
faced the flames, for strength to deal with whatever lay
in wait, for hope that no life would be lost. They knew
that material things could be replaced.

"What do you think happened?" Sarah asked. She removed the quilt from her shoulders and tucked it around
Rebecca, then sat down beside her.

"I don't know." Rebecca sounded as surprised and confused as the rest of them. "It is late. I'm sure the propane
stove was turned off. No engines would be running in the
barn at this time of night. Perhaps a kerosene lamp was
knocked over. But..." Her words trailed off, and worry
lines etched her face.

"But what?" Sarah asked.

"A kerosene lamp should not be sufficient to cause that

size flame," Sam said. His hardened features looked like they were carved in granite. He didn't seem able to pull his eyes away from the horizon. "Even if a lamp had been knocked over onto something flammable, the lamp would not have been unattended, and the resulting fire should have been easily contained."

Sarah gasped. "Are you saying this fire was deliberately set? Who would do such a thing?"

Sam stared hard at her. His silence and the truth she saw in his eyes chilled her to the bone, more than his words ever could.

"*Nee,* Samuel. I refuse to believe anyone set the fire." Rebecca rubbed her hands together against the chill that raced through her body. "In your world, you are accustomed to meeting evil every day. I understand your mind jumping to that thought. But in our community, accidents are usually just that—accidents."

Rebecca patted Sarah on the shoulder. "*Kumm* inside, child. You are still recovering and must not stress yourself. You, too, Samuel. There is nothing you can do out here to help. I will make some hot chocolate." She stood and folded the quilt over her arm. "I would appreciate it, Samuel, if you would bring in some extra wood for the fireplace. It is going to be a long night for all of us."

Rebecca stepped toward the door, but spun back around when she heard Sarah gasp.

"Look! Over there!" Sarah pointed her index finger to a spot a considerable distance west of the fire. "Do you see it? Tell me I'm not seeing what I think I see."

Sam and Rebecca huddled beside her. The three of them stared at the small flicker of light in the distance. Terrifying moments passed as they watched the light intensify and grow.

"It can't be. That's not another fire, is it?" Sarah held

her breath. She hoped it was a reflection of something, or that her overactive imagination was spooked and creating worst-case scenarios.

A second bell began clanging furiously, the frantic sound wafting across the night air.

"That's the Yoder farm." Rebecca's voice was little more than an awestruck whisper. "The Yoders have a fire."

The three of them stood in silence and watched the light quickly become an orange wall against the night.

Over the horizon and harder to see, another light appeared. Another clanging bell joined the unwanted symphony of the night.

"Oh God, please Lord, help them." Rebecca's eyes widened, and shock was evident on her face. "It is too far to be certain, but I think that is coming from Nathan and Esther's place. They just had a baby last week. Please God, let them be safe."

"Why is this happening? I don't understand." Sarah tried to keep the panic out of her voice as she counted at least three yellow-orange walls of flame shooting high in the night sky.

Sam wiped a hand over his face and then threw his arms over the shoulders of the two women huddled together in front of him.

"Evil is no longer out in the *Englisch* world, Rebecca. Evil is here."

The sunshine streaming through her bedroom window brought Sarah fully awake. She arched her back like a sleepy cat upon awakening, stretched her right arm over her head, and then used it to push up into a sitting position. She adjusted the sling on her left arm and winced at the pain still throbbing in her left shoulder whenever she jarred it.

Her thoughts wandered to the night before. Had it all been a horrible nightmare? It took her a moment to orient herself. No, it had been only too real.

She'd sat with Rebecca for hours in front of the fireplace, sipping hot chocolate, reading the Bible together and waiting. Sam had paced like a caged animal. He slipped outside every thirty minutes or so to check the Lapp barn and the perimeter of the house before hurrying back inside. He was a man whose emotions were torn. Sarah knew he'd wanted to go with Jacob and help the men, but she also knew he would never shirk his duty of protecting Rebecca and herself.

She dressed hurriedly, pulled the *kapp* over her bandaged head and walked to the bedroom door. It had been almost dawn when Jacob had come home. His body had screamed of fatigue. The haunted look in his eyes told them it had been as bad as they had suspected.

She wondered if anyone else was up yet. She eased the door open and heard the sound of men's voices below.

Padding softly down the stairs, she saw Jacob surrounded by men. She recognized Benjamin, Nathan, Thomas and several others she'd met but still couldn't place names to faces. The deep rumble of conversation wafted up the steps and then ceased when they sensed her approach.

"*Guder mariye,* gentlemen. Please don't let me interrupt." Sarah smiled and nodded as the men returned her greeting. She passed them and headed into the kitchen, stopping abruptly when she saw at least a half-dozen Amish women gathered around the table.

"*Kumm,* Sarah, join us." Rebecca waved her to the table, lifted the pot and poured her a hot cup of *kaffe*. "We are discussing the troubles of last night and dividing up the workload."

"Ya." Elizabeth Miller passed Sarah apple butter and fresh bread. "Our barn was first, but there were four more barns burned to the ground last night."

"Five barns?" Sarah couldn't keep the surprise from her voice. She'd seen three fires. There'd been two more.

"Ya, five barns. There was no way the fire department could reach even one of the barns in time, let alone five. There was nothing we could do but keep the fires from spreading," Elizabeth said.

"That's how Esther got hurt," Rebecca said. "She ran out to help Nathan. Part of the barn collapsed on her. She got a pretty nasty burn on her back."

Sarah gasped. "Isn't she the woman who just had a baby last week?"

"Ya," Rebecca replied. "We are just discussing a schedule on how we can help with chores and dinner. She will have her hands full taking care of her *boppli.* We will help with everything else until she is recovered."

"What can I do?"

"Sarah, dear, you must work on getting better yourself." Elizabeth patted her hand. "You have only been out of the hospital two days, *ya?"*

"Maybe so, but I'm not helpless. There must be something I can do, especially since…"

"What?" Elizabeth asked.

Sarah felt even worse when she saw the kindness in Elizabeth's eyes. She lowered her gaze. "Since everyone here knows it is my fault the barns were burned."

"Nonsense," Elizabeth said, and the other women at the table murmured their agreement. "You did not burn our barns. You did not hold our children hostage in their school. You did not kill one of our own and severely injure another of our loved ones." Elizabeth's eyes welled with tears. "This bad thing has happened to all of us, Sarah, and I'm thinking you have suffered most of all."

The other women at the table nodded.

"We will put this in God's hands," Rebecca said. "It is not our way to seek vengeance or punishment. It is our way to help. So let's divide the work, for there is much to do."

"Sarah and I will prepare three *yummasette* casseroles and three pies. We will deliver them to the Yoders, the Burkholders and the Zooks."

"*Gut.* Hannah and I will cook for Elizabeth and Benjamin."

Elizabeth started to protest, but Hannah waved her silent. "*Nee,* Elizabeth, you are not going to work all day, helping with Esther's house and *boppli,* and think you are coming home to your own chores, too. We will have a hot meal for you and Benjamin by the end of this day."

Elizabeth nodded. *"Danki."*

"We will all be working to help each other," Rebecca said. "Now let's finish our *kaffe.* There is much to do."

The men decided as a group to rebuild one barn at a time rather than scatter their labor force. Once that decision was made, Jacob pulled out Peter's wagon and went to town for lumber while the other men left for Benjamin's. The women scattered to their own homes to prepare the meals they'd promised.

When Rebecca returned to the kitchen, she had a surprised look on her face.

Sarah looked up from her preparations. "What? Is something missing?" She glanced down at the bread, soup, ground beef, onion, peas and noodles she had collected on the table.

Rebecca smiled. "*Nee,* everything is there. I am just happy to see you remember."

Sarah froze and then smiled. "I guess I do remember." She glanced at the ingredients in front of her and then at Rebecca. "I don't have a definite memory of making this particular casserole, but when you mentioned it I knew right away what ingredients to gather. Did I make this often?"

"One of your many talents was your cooking. After you married Peter, you took over preparing the main meal for all of us each evening. Rarely would you even let me step inside the kitchen." Rebecca smiled at her. "I suppose that is why I started making huge breakfasts for everyone."

Rebecca clasped her hand. "This is a *gut* thing, Sarah. Soon now, God willing, you will remember even more."

Sarah smiled at the older woman, but it was only a smile for show—it didn't touch her heart. Yes, she knew the ingredients for *yummasette* casserole. Just like she knew how to brush her teeth or wash her face. It came naturally to her, ingrained deep inside like breathing. But she still had no flashes of memory where she could see herself preparing the dish. She didn't want to dash Rebecca's hopes, but she was beginning to fear she would never remember the past again.

Not wanting to give Rebecca any more grief—five neighbors' barns burning through the night had caused enough of that—she squeezed the woman's hand, and the two of them began the day's cooking.

Samuel kept himself scarce for most of the day and allowed the women to work in peace. He was always on the periphery, doing what chores he could while still keeping himself within shouting distance of the kitchen. Every now and then he'd step inside under the guise of getting a glass of water. He'd snitch a piece of sliced apple or a piece of cheese, and Rebecca would puff up like a mad hen and smack at his fingers and scoot him away, but he never strayed far.

Many times through the course of the morning, Sarah could feel his eyes on her. She'd look up to see him gazing in through the kitchen window or pausing in the doorway. It should have annoyed her, but instead it made her feel cared for and protected.

Sarah sensed his discontent. She'd see him gaze in the distance toward the neighboring farms. She knew he was itching to pick up a hammer and help the men. But the moment would pass, and he'd seem to settle into his routine of barn chores and watching the women.

Samuel seemed relieved, even happy, when Rebecca asked him to hitch up the buggy so they could deliver the food.

Rebecca offered to drive the buggy herself and urged Sarah to stay behind and rest, but Sarah would have none of it. She was tired, sure. She was pretty certain they were all exhausted by now after having such little sleep. But her pain level was tolerable, and no matter what the women told her this morning, she did feel responsible for their troubles. No one would stop her from delivering this food. It was the least she could do.

Samuel sensed this. When she glanced his way, he was already standing beside the buggy and extending his hand to help her inside. They'd known each other for little more than a few weeks, and yet he seemed to know her so well—guessing correctly what she would do or how she would feel before she even knew those things herself. How could this stranger become a friend so quickly? How could they be so attuned to each other's thoughts and feelings? And what kind of pain was she going to feel when he left?

When those thoughts entered her head, she shooed them away. Samuel had become a good friend and confidant. He'd sit and talk with her for hours. Although, if she was honest, she did most of the talking.

Samuel was a great listener. He didn't judge. He didn't offer unsolicited advice. He didn't seem to expect her to be anything other than who she was. She could relax with him. She didn't have to be constantly striving to recall the past or deal with others' disappointments when she couldn't.

"Well, are you coming or do I have to carry you to the buggy?" Sam grinned and shook his waiting hand, as though she may have missed seeing it held out for the past few minutes.

"I'm coming. Hold your horses."

Sam jiggled the reins in his other hand. "That's exactly what I'm doing."

Sarah laughed and allowed him to help her into the buggy. She adjusted the basket she carried on her lap and anchored it between the sling on her left arm and her body to keep it from falling.

Sam helped Rebecca into the seat beside her, handed up the basket she carried and raced around to climb in the left side of the front seat.

"Okay, ladies. This is your last chance. Do a quick mental checklist. Do you have everything? This horse doesn't know how to turn around. It only goes forward."

Both women chuckled and assured him it was safe to leave, and he clicked his tongue and jiggled the reins.

The buggy ride was more painful than Sarah had expected. Each bounce and jolt sent shooting pains into her left shoulder and down the side of her back, but she didn't complain. She kept a smile pasted on her face and offered a silent prayer that the ride would soon be over. Gratitude washed over her when a little while later they pulled up in front of the Miller home. Benjamin's three children hooped and hollered as they raced each other to the buggy.

Rebecca nodded toward the approaching children. "You may not have your memory back yet, Sarah, but the *kinner* remember that you always bring cookies with you when you come to visit."

Samuel helped Rebecca out of the buggy. She took her basket up to the house just as William, Benjamin's oldest boy, squeezed past her into the seat she'd vacated.

"Hi, Sarah. Did you bring any chocolate chip cookies with you?"

"*Mamm* will be mad at you for asking for cookies." The little girl, who was standing on a wheel hub and leaning into the buggy, was adorable. About five or six years old with golden blond hair and brilliant blue eyes, she looked like a living, breathing doll. "But if you did bring cookies, I want one too, please."

Sarah laughed. "Well, lucky for both of you I just happen to have a fresh batch of cookies in my basket."

The children squirmed and bounced in anticipation while Sarah slipped her hand inside and pulled out one cookie for each of them. "Don't you have another brother?" She handed them their treats. "I think someone told me there are three of you."

The girl giggled, and the high-pitched melody sounded like wind chimes on a breezy day. "You're silly, Sarah. You know there are three of us—William, Daniel and me." She hung by one arm off the buggy and swung back and forth.

"You're right. How silly of me to forget." The child was so adorable. Sarah couldn't help but wonder whether her child would be a girl or a boy, and if that child would be as cute and impish as these two.

"I'll take his cookie and give it to him," William volunteered.

Sarah chuckled. Somehow she didn't think it would reach his brother without at least a little nibble out of it, if she gave the cookie to the boy.

"Where is Daniel?" she asked.

William pointed his finger. "Over there, standing by Daed and the other men in the field."

For the first time, Sarah turned her attention their way. Samuel had already joined them. She shielded her eyes from the glare of the setting sun and squinted for a better look. She noted it wasn't just Amish men standing in the field. There were two police cars parked where the rebuilding of the barn had begun, and some uniformed officers stood talking with the men. A large area of field was roped off with yellow tape.

"I wonder what's going on over there," Sarah said aloud.

"The policemen want to look at the words somebody wrote on the ground," William mumbled through a mouthful of crushed cookie.

"I don't like going over there. It's scary," the little girl said.

"It isn't scary," William corrected. "I told you, Mary, it's just spilled paint."

"Messy red paint. I don't like it. It looks like blood."

"Well, it isn't blood. It's paint. It's messy 'cause Daed said the man did it in a hurry after he set the fire in the barn."

"It's still scary. I'm gonna stay here with Sarah…and the cookies."

Her smile warmed Sarah's heart, and she had to fight the urge to pull the child close and squeeze her tight.

"Daed told us not to go over there, anyhow. He said it

was adult business and we should stay away. So I'll keep Sarah company, too…and the cookies."

Sarah reached inside the basket. "Okay. You win. I can't resist your beautiful smiles. You can have another cookie."

After handing them another cookie each, she glanced over again at the men. "William, do you know what words the man wrote in red paint?"

"*Ya,* but they didn't make any sense." He bit his cookie.

"Why don't you tell me? Maybe they'll make sense to me."

"It was only four words. I don't know why everyone is so upset about them."

"What did the words say?"

He swallowed his last bite of cookie and then said, "'Give her to me.'"

ELEVEN

Sarah gasped and then, not wanting to upset the children, she pretended to cough. "Well, *danki*. Go play now. Shoo. I have to get these goodies in the house while I still have some left."

She slid across the seat, but before she could attempt to climb out of the buggy, Sam had returned and was standing below her. He took the basket out of her hand and placed it on the ground. Instead of offering his hand, he clasped her waist and lifted her high, as if she were as light as a flower in the breeze. Heat seared her cheeks as the firm touch of his hands on her waist sent her pulse flying. The heat deepened when she stared into his eyes and saw he knew the effect he was having on her.

"Danki," she said when he placed her on the ground. Trying to hide her reaction to his nearness, she glanced over at the men still gathered by the field. "William told me about the words written in the field."

Sam picked up her basket, clasped her right arm with his hand and guided her toward the house. "This is why I became a police officer in the first place. The Amish people are not accustomed to the evil that exists in the world."

"And you are?"

He stopped midstride and shot a look her way. "Yes,

Sarah. I have met evil face-to-face many times. The Amish are my people. I chose to devote my life to protecting them because they are peaceful people who will not protect themselves."

"They depend on God for protection, Samuel. Certainly you do not think you are God?"

The words sounded harsh even to her own ears, and instantly she wished she could recall them. She hadn't meant to be unkind. She was just trying to understand what drove a man who loved God, his family and his people to leave them behind.

Sam's hand tightened on her arm, and his body bristled. The red flush on his throat was the only physical sign that she had hit a nerve, and it had angered him. "No, Sarah, I know I am not God." He gestured toward the field. "But He seems to be a little busy someplace else right now, so I thought I'd give Him a hand."

She knew she couldn't take back what she had said or soften its blow, so she continued walking beside him in silence.

"There they are." Rebecca's voice carried on the air. "See, I told you they were right behind me." Rebecca and Elizabeth peered from the doorway and beckoned them inside.

Sam handed the basket to Elizabeth and spoke to Rebecca. "I'll leave Sarah in your safe hands."

Even though his words were light, Sarah knew Samuel well enough by now to feel the anger emanating from him. He didn't even glance in her direction as he marched off to rejoin the men.

Sarah gazed at his back as he moved farther away, and wished she could rewind the past few minutes and eat her words. Since she couldn't, she followed the other two women into the house and vowed to apologize to him later when they could find a moment or two alone.

But the time never presented itself.

The afternoon slipped into evening in a flurry of activity. Jacob and Rebecca drove the buggy home with Sarah in the second seat while Sam brought up the rear with the lumber wagon.

The next few days fell into a similar pattern. The women cooked all morning, delivered the food to various farms in the afternoons, helped with cleanup and returned early evening just in time to finish their own chores, say their prayers, get some sleep and do it all over again.

Their visit to the Yoder farm had the most impact on Sarah. With her left arm still in a sling, she wasn't able to cradle and rock the Yoders' new infant as the other women did. But she had managed to steal a private moment with the newborn.

Sarah couldn't resist tracing her finger across the silken softness of the baby's cheek, and a smile tugged at the corner of her mouth at the strength of the fisted hold the child had on her finger. She counted the ten perfect little fingers and ten perfect little toes. She watched the tiny lips pucker in a sucking motion as the baby slept. She breathed in the clean, fresh baby-powder scent and, for the first time, longed for the day when she would be hovering over the cradle of her own child.

Almost as if the child she carried could read her mind, Sarah felt a slight stirring, like butterfly wings fluttering in her stomach, and she knew this was her baby moving about, letting her know it wasn't a story a doctor had made up, but that this child was very real and would soon be in her arms.

The thought comforted her—and frightened her, as well. She didn't know the first thing about giving birth or raising a child. And she would have to do it alone, without a husband to help and guide her.

Raising a child would be the most important job she would ever have. She offered a silent prayer that God would be with her each step of the way so she could raise the child in the ways of the Lord—with love and patience, without fear or self-doubt.

"Sarah?"

She spun around at the sound of Sam's voice.

"I'm sorry. I didn't mean to startle you." He stood a few feet from her and held his hat in his hand. He glanced at the baby in the cradle and then looked back at her. It was as if he could look into her mind, into her very soul, and he smiled. "Soon you will have a *boppli* of your own. That is exciting, *ya?*"

His features scrunched up as he studied her, but after a moment, a slight smile teased his lips. "I know life has been hard for you lately, but we will find this man. This will be over soon, and you will be happy again. I promise."

"Only God can promise such things, Samuel." Before he could respond, she raised a hand to stop him. "I apologize for the harshness of my words a few days ago. I did not mean to insult you by implying you thought yourself like God. I do not think such a sinful thing, or think you are prideful."

She softened her voice. "I was just trying to understand why you made the choices you did. And if you ever regretted those choices." She lowered her eyes.

Sam tilted her chin and looked into her face. "I had my reasons for leaving, Sarah. Good reasons. And no…I do not regret the choice I made. I am no longer Amish, and I will never return to this way of life. My time here will end when my job is over."

Sarah's heart clenched. She didn't want to be reminded

that he was only here for a short time. She didn't want to imagine how empty her days would be without seeing him at work in the barn or sitting across from her at the dinner table. She didn't want to think what it would be like not to sit beside him in the evenings and count the stars. Not to have him near so they could talk.

So she wouldn't think about it. For now she would pretend that he would always be here—and she'd deal with the pain later, when he left.

"What is so important, Samuel, that you sneak up behind me and startle me to death?"

He grinned. "Rebecca asked me to fetch you. She went to join Jacob in the buggy. They are ready to go home."

"Well, why didn't you say so?" She brushed past him in a huff, unable to hide her annoyance. It wasn't his delay in telling her that Rebecca was waiting for her that bothered her. It was the fact that no matter how much she wanted to or how hard she tried, she couldn't forget that soon Samuel would leave.

Sarah gazed out the window. The skies were gray, and the smell of rain was in the air.

The sun did its best to break through the clouds but was losing the battle. It would be dusk soon, and the men would be coming home, looking for a hot dinner and a good night's rest.

She pressed her face against the windowpane. She should be able to see Samuel from here. He'd told her he wouldn't go far. He needed to help Jacob mend some downed fencing before the worst of the impending storm hit, but the barn obstructed her view.

Samuel had not said anything else about leaving since their discussion a couple of days ago. But the subject hung in the air between them. She knew he saw the sadness in her eyes when she looked at him, but she couldn't help it. He had become a dear and close friend. Why would she be happy about his going?

Sarah was pretty certain that Samuel wasn't happy about going, either. She had seen a deep, pensive expression on his face more than once when he thought she wasn't looking. She knew she wasn't imagining it. Samuel liked her, too. They had become friends.

And friends harbored a fondness for each other.

Friends would miss friends if they parted.

And sometimes…friendships deepened. Feelings grew. If Samuel started having deeper feelings, it might be hard for him to say goodbye. Right? She could only hope…and wait…and pray.

She rubbed her hand against the glass, trying to erase the moisture her warm breath had caused on the cold pane. Still no sight of him. She had to stop acting like a mooning teenager and get downstairs and help Rebecca with dinner.

She noticed that she had more fluid movements these days. She wasn't due to see the doctor again for a couple of days, but she was optimistic about the visit. She knew her body was healing. She didn't tire as easily. Her pain had lessened, and she was looking forward to getting the sling off her left arm and the bandages off her head. All she wanted to do was soak in a hot bath and shampoo her hair. Who would have thought that the idea of such a small thing promised so much pleasure?

"I was just going to call you." Rebecca, her face flushed from standing over the hot stove, waved her over. "I need to go out to the barn. I forgot to bring in the pickled beets and corn. The bread is rising nicely but needs to be watched. The stew needs to be stirred. Will you please watch the meal? I will be right in."

Sarah gestured for her to stay where she was and

grabbed her sweater hanging on the hook by the front door. "You're the cook. Who better to tend the food? I'll fetch what you need."

"Are you sure? It's going to start pouring any minute."

"Yes, I'm sure. I've been looking forward to catching raindrops on my tongue."

Rebecca laughed. "I must be getting old. That thought never entered my mind."

Sarah smiled back. "Do you need anything else while I'm out there?"

"Will you be able to carry more than two Mason jars with just the use of one arm?"

"Of course."

"*Gut,* then please bring me a jar of sliced apples, too."

Sarah nodded and hurried out the door before Rebecca could change her mind. She stopped midway between the house and barn and lifted her face to the sky. Thick, dark clouds were rolling in rapidly. A breeze caught the leaves of the trees and teased the dust of the ground into swirls around her feet.

Maybe spring was one of her favorite seasons. She didn't have any specific memories to draw from so it was only a guess, but she was pretty sure she was right. She loved the smell of freshly cut grass, the flowering buds that poked their heads through the last of the winter's snows, the warmth of the day followed by the chill of evening where she would sit in front of a roaring fire and sip a cup of hot chocolate.

Samuel was right. If she still couldn't recover memories of the past, she could decide what pleased her now and form new memories for the future. Today she decided that spring was definitely her favorite season.

She unlatched the barn door. Before she opened it, a

sound caught her attention and made her pause. She looked over her shoulder. Had Jacob and Samuel returned?

She couldn't see anyone, but an inner awareness told her that she wasn't alone.

"Hello. Is anybody there?"

Her words were swallowed up in the impending storm. She squinted her eyes and tried to focus as she let her gaze wander around the yard. Darkness was descending on the farmyard and the first, fat drops of rain began plopping on the ground. She knew she needed to hurry with her task, find the items and get back to the house before Rebecca started to worry. But still she hesitated. Her senses told her she was being watched, even if her eyes didn't see anyone.

"Samuel? Jacob?" she called out as loudly as she could. Nothing but silence.

Apprehension crept up her spine.

Hurriedly, she let herself into the barn. The wind had picked up, and she had to exert all her energy to pull the door shut behind her. She briskly walked to the pantry in the far corner of the barn, opened the doors and started to search the shelves for the items. So much food. Rebecca must have cooked and canned all last summer. She had enough stored in here to feed an army.

But of course, being the bishop, Jacob often had people to the house for a variety of reasons. He likely presided over weddings, counseled those in need, met with the elders of the church and occasionally took his turn conducting church services. Plus, Rebecca had told her that she often delivered food to the sick and shut-ins throughout the year.

Sarah found the beets and corn quickly. It took a few minutes more to find the apples since Rebecca had jars of pears, peaches and a variety of berries, as well. She slipped two of the jars inside her sling and grinned at how she was finding many other uses for this sling besides just holding a useless arm. With the third jar clasped in her right hand, she shoved the pantry door shut with her forearm.

She had turned to go back to the house when the sound of metal upon metal froze her in place. Someone tinkered with the handle of the barn door.

"Hello? Jacob? Samuel?"

Someone was out there. It was probably one of them, but why hadn't they answered when she called?

The barn door swung open, and a man stepped inside. She knew with just one glance that this wasn't anyone who should be here this late in the day. This man's dress was *Englisch* .

A shiver of anxiety shook her from head to toe. Why was a complete stranger standing in their barn in the middle of an impending thunderstorm? Panic made her want to run. Logic and common sense kept her calm and standing in place. There had to be a simple explanation.

The storm! That must be it. Perhaps he was afraid he couldn't outrun the storm, and he wanted someplace safe to wait for it to pass. Or maybe he had lost his way and just wanted directions to town. No reason to panic.

"Can I help you?"

The man didn't reply but, instead, took several strides in her direction. Just as quickly, Sarah stepped back. Something was wrong. This man didn't belong here, and he wasn't answering any of her questions.

Her heart thundered in her chest.

Please God, help me. Is this the man who burned the barns? Who killed Peter and shot me? Has he come to kill me?

"Who are you?" She tried not to reveal her terror, but her voice betrayed her.

The man sprinted forward.

Startled by his actions, Sarah dropped the jar from her hand and cried out. She turned and ran toward the back door of the barn. She had almost reached it when she lost her footing and tumbled onto the barn floor. The impact of her body on the barn floor broke the jars hidden in her sling. Glass sliced her skin. The force of the fall shot fresh pain radiating through her arm and shooting into her shoulder.

Dear Lord, protect my child. Please don't let this man kill me.

Stifling a groan, she rolled onto her back to face her assailant. She wouldn't go easily. She intended to fight for her life—for her child's life.

But it was too late. The stranger loomed over her, and she was unable to get to her feet or run. Something was in his hand, but he moved it too quickly for her to identify it.

Please Lord, don't let it be a gun.

The man raised his hand high and pointed the object at her.

She flung her arm up to protect her face, squeezed her eyes closed and screamed.

TWELVE

Sarah tried to prepare herself for the sound of gunfire and the slamming pain she expected at any moment from bullets entering her body. Still, she refused to give up. She crab walked on her back as quickly as she could in a last-ditch attempt to scurry away from the stranger.

Instead of gunfire, she heard a muffled *oomph*.

Sarah opened her eyes and couldn't believe what she saw. As if caught in a tornado, the stranger was lifted straight up into the air. His body flew several feet to her right and slammed hard into one of the barn's support beams. She leaned up on her elbows for a closer look, but before she could react she felt hands pulling on the back of her arms.

"*Kumm,* Sarah, let me help you." Jacob helped her to her feet. "Are you all right? Did he hurt you?"

Sarah brushed at her clothing. "I'm fine, Jacob. Just scared."

The sound of a strangled scream caught their attention, and both of them hurried toward the stranger.

"*Nee,* Samuel, don't." Jacob tried to pull Sam's hands off the man. Samuel had a fisted hold on some kind of binding around the man's neck and was holding the stranger several inches off the ground by it. The man looked terrified, his face red, eyes bulging, breath coming in gasps.

"Stop, Samuel. Let him go." Jacob tried to insert his body between them. "This is not our way."

With a ferocity that Sarah had never witnessed before, Sam pushed Jacob away and refused to release his hold on the stranger. "I am not one of you. Remember? This is my way, so step back."

Sarah rushed forward and gently placed her hand on Sam's shoulder. "But is it God's way, Samuel?"

Sarah wasn't sure whether it was the truth of her words, the sound of her voice or her touch, but Sam froze. He seemed to struggle for a few minutes with his anger, but gradually gained control. He released the hold on the binding around the man's neck and let him fall to his feet. The stranger doubled at the waist and coughed and gasped for breath.

"Who are you?" Sam loomed over the man. His tone of voice threatened more violence if he didn't receive the answers he wanted.

"Roger...Roger Mathers." The stranger started to reach inside his pocket.

Sam drew his weapon with lightning speed and had it aimed at point-blank range at the man's chest before the gasp left Sarah's lips.

"Don't move," he ordered.

The stranger did as he was told. "I was just going to show you my credentials." His voice trembled.

"Do it slow and easy." Sam's tone of voice and stern expression brooked no hesitation.

Roger pulled out a plastic card with his photograph and name printed on it. His fingers trembled as he offered it to Sam, who snatched it from his grasp and read it.

"A reporter? I don't believe it." He threw the identification back at the man. It bounced off his chest and landed on the dirt floor. "You're working for a sleazebag tabloid?" Sam muttered something unintelligible under his breath. "What are you doing sneaking around out here?"

"I'm sorry. I didn't mean any harm. Do you know how much money I could get for an exclusive picture? Everyone knows the Amish don't like their pictures taken. But a picture like this one..." He hung his head. "My wife's sick. I need the money."

For the first time, Sarah took a good look at the man. She saw the camera hanging from a thick cord at his neck. That's what he'd pointed at her—a camera, not a gun. A wave of relief flowed over her. She noted the bright red marks on the man's neck from the camera strap and felt sorry for him. "What is wrong with your wife?"

"She needs an operation." He looked hopeful. "Just one picture would guarantee that for me."

Sam grabbed the man and slammed him back against the wood. "Knock it off, Mathers. Stop trying to play on her sympathies, you creep. You don't have a sick wife. Tell them the truth." He knocked him back again. "Tell them."

"Okay!" He raised his hands. "So I don't have a wife. So what? Get your hands off me before I press charges."

"Call the sheriff. Go for it. I'd love to see what happens when a trespasser calls in to report his own crime."

Mathers's face contorted into an angry grimace, and he swatted Sam's hands away.

Sarah's mouth fell open. No wife? No operation? How could a person lie so convincingly? Worse, how much evil had Samuel witnessed that he would recognize it so quickly and easily?

Jacob had remained silent through it all, but now Sarah heard low murmured prayers behind her. Apparently, Jacob was uncomfortable in the presence of evil, too.

"How did you find her?" Sam folded his arms over his chest and returned the glare.

"Easy." He moved his hand toward his inside coat pocket, waited for Sam to nod permission and pulled out a folded paper. "The dry-goods store sells these church directories."

Sam took the paper from his hand and looked it over, then he glanced at Jacob. "Why didn't you tell me about this? This paper not only has all the names and addresses of everyone in the community, but it also has a map to each farm."

Jacob blinked and looked confused. "Of course. Many Amish communities publish this information. We do not want anyone who wishes to attend a church service to get lost or to forget who is having the service that particular week." Jacob looked puzzled. "Have you been gone so long, Samuel, that you forgot something as common and simple as this?"

A flush of red crept up Sam's neck. Instead of responding to Jacob, he grabbed Mathers by his coat collar and shoved him toward the door. "Get out of here. Don't set foot on this property again, or you'll get more than my hands on you. I guarantee I'll be the one calling the sheriff. You'll have a one-way handcuffed trip to jail for trespassing on private property."

Without a backward glance, Mathers ran out of the barn.

Sam watched Mathers's back. Not because he wanted to make sure the man was gone. Like the cockroach he was, he knew the man would scurry into the night. No, he needed the few precious moments to gain control of his emotions before he could turn and face Sarah.

The sound of her screams still echoed in his head. His

heart hammered in his chest. Adrenaline raced through his blood.

"What's going on? Who was that man?" Rebecca, her coat flapping open and her *kapp* askew, rushed into the barn. "Is everything all right? I came out to check when Sarah hadn't returned."

Jacob slid his arm over Rebecca's shoulders and pulled her close. "*Ya,* everything is as it should be. We are all fine and hungry. Ain't so, Samuel?"

Sam didn't respond. Instead, he turned toward Sarah. He knew he shouldn't, but he couldn't stop himself. As if in a slow-motion movie, he reached out and drew her to him. His arms encircled her waist. He felt her cheek press against his chest. With his left hand, he cradled the top of her head against him.

"Sarah…" It was all he could say—and it said everything. The anguish, the fear, the concern. His emotions coated his words, and there was no hiding the feelings behind them.

Rebecca gasped at the sight of the sudden intimacy.

"Samuel." Jacob's voice was firm and censuring.

Sam couldn't process Jacob's words or his tone. All he could think about was how close he'd come to losing her—again.

"When I saw that man standing over you, it was like a switch went off inside of me, and all I felt was rage." Samuel loosened his hold enough to let her move a step back. "Not just for the threat he presented. But mostly at myself, I think, because I let you down again."

"Shh." Sarah placed her fingertips on his lips and looked into his eyes. "You did not let me down, Samuel. You saved me."

The shimmering in her brilliant blue eyes and the smile on her perfectly shaped lips clenched his heart as tightly as if it were squeezed in an iron fist. He was developing feelings for this woman. He couldn't deny it anymore to anyone, not even himself.

But he couldn't let it continue.

He was her bodyguard. Her protector. He had to keep his emotions in check, his mind sharp so he'd be able to do the job. There was a definite, though invisible, line drawn between every bodyguard and victim, a line he couldn't cross. Not now. Not ever.

And in Sarah's case, it was more than a line. It was a canyon-size gorge, impossible to bridge. She was a pregnant, vulnerable *Amish* widow. He was an *Englischer* who would return to a world that held no place for the sweetness or softness of Sarah. Whether he harbored feelings for her was no longer the question. He did. But if he didn't want to hurt her, he had to bury those feelings. Permanently. Right now.

"Samuel!" This time Jacob's voice demanded attention. When Sam looked at him, he said, "Rebecca can tend to Sarah. We should go into the house and clean up for dinner."

Their eyes met. Jacob's gaze was stern, clearly showing displeasure in the inappropriate affection Sam had just shown Sarah. Sam's eyes held both shame for dishonoring these kind people, as well as challenge that he wasn't able to express his heart.

It was Rebecca's gaze that made him feel guilt and hang his head. She looked shocked and disappointed and wary...as if a trust had been broken. And it had.

"Kumm." Rebecca rushed past him to Sarah's side. "I don't know what happened, but you can tell me all about it while we get dinner on the table."

Sarah glanced down at her soiled sling and dress. "I'm so sorry, Rebecca. I broke the Mason jars when I fell."

"Were you hurt?"

"I banged my shoulder pretty hard." She grinned humorously. "Just when the pain went away, now it is back again."

"Let's go inside. We'll get you in dry clothes and make sure you didn't do more damage to yourself. It is a good thing you are scheduled to see Dr. Clark in the morning. He will fix you up good as new."

"But the vegetables…"

"It doesn't matter. We have more. Jacob, please bring in some corn and beets." Wrapping her arm around Sarah's shoulders, she ushered her toward the house, but not before shooting a warning glance at Sam that said it all.

Stand back. Keep away. She belongs to us, not you.

And she was right.

Jacob didn't say anything. He didn't have to. He handed Sam a Mason jar, clapped his hand a couple of times on his back as though consoling him, and then the two men walked in silence to the house.

The following morning Sam offered his hand to Rebecca and helped her out of the back of the car. He wished he'd been able to be the driver that morning when he'd accompanied the women to see Dr. Clark. It would have made the trip go faster and less stressful.

He was sure his cover had been blown, anyway. News travels quickly in an Amish community, and he could tell from the nods and glances sent his way that everyone knew by now who and what he was. It also stood to reason that the stranger in town who'd been seeking Sarah and the "man protecting her" had a pretty good idea that he was a cop and not an Amish farmer.

But undercover meant *undercover*. Until they were certain his cover was no longer in place, he had to act as if it were.

So he had climbed into the backseat and let one of the other police officers act as driver today. He'd been smart and had made sure to sit between the door and Rebecca, setting himself an acceptable distance from Sarah. He had no desire to endure another day of sharp, disapproving glances from Rebecca as he had through dinner last night. It seemed to work. The less attention he gave Sarah, the more Rebecca relaxed.

Once Rebecca exited, he turned to offer a hand to Sarah. He kept his face an unreadable mask. He was certain no one could see in his expression just how lovely he thought Sarah's blond hair looked now that the bandages had been removed from her head. Even tucked beneath her white *kapp,* enough errant strands escaped to glisten like gold and make his fingers itch to see if it felt as silky as it looked.

He didn't allow a smile to cross his lips when, free of the sling she no longer had to wear, she stretched her left arm across the back of the seat.

And he was particularly careful to keep any tenderness out of his eyes when he noted how her dress stretched across the growing swell of her body as she scooted across the seat.

"*Danki,* Samuel." She smiled that beautiful, sweet smile of hers and he thought he'd melt at her feet. Before he made a fool of himself, she turned away.

Jacob met them in the yard with a horse already hitched to a wagon and waiting.

"Are we going to Nathan Yoder's house now?" Sarah asked when she saw him. "It's our day to help with the *boppli* and the housework, isn't it?"

"*Nee,* it is my day to help," Rebecca replied. "You had

a long trip back and forth to the city today. You heard what the doctor said. You are healing nicely and getting stronger, but you need more rest. He does not want you to overdo it."

"But…"

"You can be helpful without coming with me."

Sarah gave her a questioning look.

"It would be *wunderbaar* to come home to a hot meal. I have a pot of stew that needs tending."

"That is not much of a chore, Rebecca, to stir a pot of stew every now and then."

"Your job today is to rest. You can work your fingers to the bone tomorrow."

Jacob finished loading the back of the wagon with supplies. "*Ya,* Sarah. I would appreciate a hot bowl of stew when I finish the repairs on Nathan's barn. I understand that, to you, it does not seem like much of a chore. To us, it is a task we hope you will do well because we will be looking forward to the rewards all day."

The small group laughed. Sarah nodded and threw up her hands in surrender. "Okay, Jacob. I will stir the stew."

"Danki." Jacob helped Rebecca into the wagon.

Sarah watched them pull away. "Be sure to kiss the *boppli* for me," she yelled as the wagon moved down the lane. Her words were answered with a wave from both of them.

"Should we go into the house?" Sam stood near the porch steps and waited.

"Nee, Samuel. I need you to prepare the buggy for me. I'm going into town."

Sam frowned at her but refrained from offering what he knew would be a useless argument. When Sarah set her mind on something, she was not easily swayed from doing it.

"Where are we going?" he asked.

Sarah opened her mouth to speak and then shut it. "I don't suppose I could convince you to stay behind?"

Sam scowled.

"I didn't think so. We're going into town. A hot, steamy stew should be accompanied by a hot, sweet dessert. I found a wonderful recipe in a cookbook I was looking at the other day. I want to try it, but Rebecca does not have all the necessary ingredients."

"Dessert. Ah, you found my soft spot. I'll have the horse hitched up in no time."

"Good. But we must hurry. I need to get back in plenty of time to tend the stew and make the dessert."

They rode in companionable silence for a good part of the journey. The brisk morning air kissed her cheeks, but she enjoyed the feel of the fresh breeze against her skin. The billowing, uncut grass in the meadows and the bare tree branches rapidly being clothed with green leaves made her smile. She thanked God for such a beautiful day.

"Are you going to give me a hint about what kind of dessert you'll be making?" Sam grinned at her.

"Nee."

"No? You'd really torture me like that? I'm sitting here thinking up one thing after another, each one better than before, and my stomach is growling. Can't you hear it?"

"I won't tell you, but you can try to guess."

He laughed, and the deep rumble in his throat made Sarah's smile widen.

"A homemade cherry pie," he guessed.

"Nee."

"No? Then pumpkin. Or sweet potato, maybe."

"Not even close."

"Apples. You're making crisp apple strudel or baked apples and cream."

Sarah shook her head.

"Give me a hint."

"We are not shopping for fruit, Samuel. Rebecca has more than enough. I need chocolate and heavy cream and marshmallows and—"

Before she could finish, Sam grabbed at his chest as if he was having a heart attack. "Oh, you're killing me. I love chocolate. I am a chocolate fool. It's my deep, dark secret that I can be easily manipulated with just the promise of chocolate."

Sarah giggled at the silliness of their game. But then Samuel always brought a smile to her face, made her feel happy and content, sometimes by doing nothing more than walking through a door.

Suddenly, their horse flung her head in the air and moved slightly right and then left.

Sam stopped the teasing banter and turned his attention to the horse. He tightened his grip on the reins and spoke to the mare. "Easy, girl. Take it easy."

The horse tossed its head again and whinnied.

"Something is spooking her." Sarah checked both the road ahead and the landscape. "I don't see anything that should be frightening her."

Sam pulled back on the reins and continued speaking in a calm, soothing voice. "Whoa, girl. Quiet down. You're okay." He slowed the mare from a brisk trot to a steady walk.

Within seconds, the roar of a car engine sounded behind them.

"What the…" Sam threw a glance over his shoulder and then turned back to soothe the horse, who grew more agitated as the car approached.

"That car is going awfully fast." Sarah clasped the frame of the window and leaned her head out for a closer look. "But Molly shouldn't be scared. She's used to cars on the road."

The driver of the car revved the engine and sped even faster toward them.

"This one isn't operating like the normal drivers Molly is used to," Sam said. "No wonder she's spooked. The fool shouldn't be speeding on a country road like this. It's dangerous." Samuel edged the mare to the side of the road, being sure to leave plenty of space for the car to pass, and then brought the buggy to a stop. "Let's wait and let him go by."

Within seconds the car flew past. His tires spewed an arc of gravel and dust. Samuel ducked as he was pummeled with the spray. Although Sarah couldn't hear the words he muttered under his breath, she was certain he wasn't happy.

Once the car passed, Sam made a clicking sound with his mouth, bounced the reins and eased Molly and the buggy back onto the lane. They'd gone only a few dozen yards when Molly stopped dead in her tracks and whinnied loudly.

One look told Sarah all she needed to know. "Samuel." Her blood froze in her veins. She tried to keep the anxiety out of her voice when she spoke. "He's coming back. Why would he be coming back?"

Sam didn't answer. By now he had done all he could do to control the frightened horse. Again he moved them to the shoulder of the road, and again the car rushed past at a dangerous, accelerated speed, veering toward them like a bull charging a matador.

"Did you see the driver?" Sam asked. The set of his square jaw and a grim frown on his face revealed his own tension regarding this strange and unforeseen situation. "Could it be teenagers playing a dangerous prank?"

"I don't think so, Samuel." Sarah strained her neck to see behind them. "I'm certain I only saw one man in the car."

Within seconds the car came back—faster, closer, more threatening. This time the side of the car actually scraped against the buggy. Molly whinnied, pawed the earth and tried to run to the right. Samuel struggled to keep control of the terrified animal. While he fought with the reins, he yelled, "Get my cell phone out of my pocket. Hurry!"

Sarah didn't hesitate. She scooted over as close as she could get, allowed her hand to slide across the warmth of his chest until she located the small cell phone tucked in the pocket of his shirt. She withdrew it immediately and held it in an outstretched palm.

Once Molly had calmed, Sam chanced loosening his grip on the reins and grabbed the phone out of her hand. Within seconds he had called his sergeant, given their location and asked for immediate backup.

But the call was too late.

Sarah watched in horror, unable to believe her eyes. The car crested the rise and increased its speed until it seemed to be flying. Sarah clutched his sleeve and pointed. "Samuel, look. He's driving right at us!"

Already pulled as far off the road as possible, Samuel had nowhere else to go. The car was to their left and closing the distance between them. The horse, against the fence to their right, whinnied in fear. She reared to her hind legs in panic.

"Get out!" Samuel yelled and pushed hard. She fell between the buggy and the fence.

The horse reared to her hind legs. Seconds later the

car smashed into the buggy. Sam flew through the air and landed with such force, he momentarily blacked out.

When he opened his eyes, he pulled himself to a sitting position. He grabbed his head in an attempt to stop the waves of pain and dizziness trying to claim him. Taking a deep breath, he dared to look at the carnage. His brain didn't seem to want to register what he saw. Pieces of buggy were strewn all over the road and well into the fields on both sides of the lane. The car, although it must have sustained considerable damage, had managed to drive off and was out of sight.

Sam scrambled to his feet, stumbling and half running toward the fence. He stopped abruptly when he was only a few steps away, an expression of relief on his face which was immediately replaced by one of anxiety.

Tears streamed down Sarah's face.

"Sarah? Are you all right?" He stepped closer but didn't touch her.

Sarah laughed uncontrollably and she could see by Sam's expression that he didn't know what to make of it but she couldn't stop. Her anxiety level was high and the laughter seemed to be her body's way of coping.

"Look!" Sarah pointed toward Molly, and a fresh wave of giggles erupted from her. "Molly is ready to take us home."

Sam looked in the direction she pointed. The horse stood docilely by, still in harness. The remnants of what was left of the front seat of the buggy were wrapped in the reins. To a passerby, it would look like the horse forgot the buggy altogether and waited for her master to take their seats so she could pull them home.

Sarah took a second glance at him and came to his side instantly. "You're hurt."

"It's just a scratch."

She probed his wound. The soft, feathery touch of her fingers against the heat of his skin was almost his undoing. He clasped her wrist and stilled her hand.

Their eyes locked. Sam thought he would never be able to pull his gaze away from the glistening blue pools staring back at him. Her lips were slightly parted and only a breath out of reach—and he wanted to reach, to taste, to lose himself in a stolen, forbidden kiss.

"Samuel?" The whisper of his name on her lips brought him back to sanity. He was her bodyguard, her protector, and he couldn't let himself pretend or even hope for one moment that he could be anything else.

"It's just a bump." The huskiness in his voice made a lie of his sudden aloofness. But still, he had to try. "How about you? Are you okay? Are you hurt?"

Sarah stared hard at him, searching his face for something, an answer to an unasked question that hung in the air between them. Slowly she smiled—a sad smile, an understanding smile—and she withdrew her wrist from his grasp.

"I'm fine," she whispered.

He knew she didn't understand his emotional withdrawal, and a deep, clenching pain seized his heart with the knowledge that he was causing her pain. But he had a job to do—and a different world to go home to.

Turning away, Sarah crossed the few feet to her horse and lovingly stroked the mare's neck. "Good girl, Molly." She ran her hand along the animal's back and crouched down to run her fingers over all four legs. When she seemed satisfied that Molly was uninjured, she looked over her shoulder at him.

"Why, Samuel?" Her face still wet with tears, her laughter faded to hiccuping breaths. "Poor Molly could have been hurt or worse. We could have been killed. Why would anyone do such a careless thing?"

"It was not careless, Sarah. It was deliberate and premeditated. Just like the shooting in the schoolhouse. Just like the fires on the farms."

He withdrew his gun from his shoulder holster.

"What are you doing?" Sarah looked at the weapon in his hand as if he held a poisonous snake.

"I won't be caught unprepared again. I never should have agreed to Jacob's terms. I will no longer carry an empty gun for fear of offending Amish sensibilities."

"No, Samuel, please. There must be another way." She choked and had difficulty forcing out her words.

The pain on her face seized his heart and made it difficult for him to draw a breath. Right now he hated himself for what he knew she must be thinking of him. She was seeing a side of him she'd heard about, knew existed, but until now hadn't seen.

She straightened and stared hard at him.

"Violence is never the Amish way, Samuel."

He broke his gaze away from her pleading eyes and slammed the clip into the base of the weapon.

"I've told you before, Sarah. I am not Amish. Not anymore. Not ever again."

THIRTEEN

Captain Rogers offered Sam a cup of hot coffee. Sam was pretty sure it had been the captain's coffee, but he accepted it gratefully.

"That's a pretty good knot on your forehead. Maybe you should get it checked out. I can put someone else on Sarah's protection detail until you get back."

Sam glanced across the dozen yards that separated him from Sarah. Past the local police and state trooper cars. Past the flashing strobe lights. Finally resting on the ambulance that had pulled up a short time ago.

He could see Sarah sitting in the back as the paramedics checked her out. He'd done a cursory check of her before they'd arrived, and other than suffering a few bumps and bruises from being thrown out of the buggy, she appeared physically fine.

Emotionally, however? She hadn't spoken a word to him since he'd loaded his weapon, and he couldn't help but wonder if she ever would again.

He couldn't erase the memory of the look on Sarah's face. For the first time since they'd met, the reality of what he did for a living had seemed to come crashing down on her. She'd seen him in cop mode, gun in hand, ready to kill—and her look of horror pierced his soul.

"Sam? Did you hear me? Are you okay?"

"Yes, Captain. I heard you and I'm fine. No need to replace me. Thanks."

"Did you see who did it?"

"No. It happened too fast, and I needed to focus my attention on controlling the horse. I couldn't get a license plate number. It was a dark blue sedan. Didn't look like a foreign model, and probably wasn't more than a year or two old. What I am sure about is that the perp held pedal to the metal. This was deliberate." He dumped out what was left in his cup. "Sarah confirmed that it was a sole driver."

Captain Rogers nodded. "Luckily I'd driven up from the city this morning to take a look at the situation for myself. I was with the sheriff when the call came in. We set up roadblocks the second you called it in. He put out a BOLO for any car in the area with body damage, but so far it hasn't turned up anything."

"We both know it was our guy."

Rogers planted his hands on his hips. The scowl on his face as he stared out over the accident scene said it all.

"He's leaving bodies in his wake, and we can't touch him." His superior scratched his head. "He burned down five local barns in one night. He attacked the two of you on the road. And he's still a ghost. No name. No picture. No leads." He rubbed a hand across his face. "He's a cocky character. Always one step ahead of us. No question he knows we've got state troopers, local police and undercover officers in place. Nothing deters him. He's fearless."

"We'll see how fearless he is once I get my hands on him."

"Is that your brain talking, King, or your emotions?" Captain Rodgers clapped a hand on Sam's shoulder. "You've got to keep your wits about you if you're going to catch this guy. He's smart, Sam…and deadly."

"You think?" Sam laughed mirthlessly. "He administered an almost lethal dose of potassium to Sarah right under my nose. He killed the relief cop guarding her door. He killed my partner. You think I don't know the evil I'm dealing with?"

Captain Rogers returned a hard, steady gaze. "Evil, huh? You know, I've never discussed your religious beliefs with you before, Sam. But this time you might be right. If we are dealing with evil personified, it wouldn't hurt if you took a moment and had a conversation with the man upstairs. We sure could use some help on this one."

Rogers walked back to join the sheriff just as Jacob and Rebecca's buggy pulled up.

The two of them spoke briefly to one of the officers, and then Rebecca raced to the back of the ambulance. After another short conversation with the paramedics, Rebecca wrapped her arm around Sarah and ushered her to their buggy. Before she climbed on board, Sarah threw a glance over her shoulder and her gaze locked with his. Without a word, she climbed into the buggy.

Jacob followed her gaze, spotted Sam and walked over to where he stood.

"You've been hurt."

"It's nothing."

The man studied his face, looked as if he was going to argue that statement and then decided to keep his counsel.

"Please, can you take Sarah home? She's been through a lot and must be exhausted." When Jacob turned to go, Sam clasped his arm. "Make sure you ask the sheriff to send one of his men with you until I finish up here and can get back. And Jacob, keep Sarah inside the house. Period."

Jacob nodded and walked briskly back to the buggy. A police cruiser, lights flashing, pulled out and slowly

followed the buggy as it turned and headed back the way
it had come.

Sam stood at the side of the lane and watched until they
disappeared over the rise. He couldn't erase the memory
of what he'd seen in Sarah's eyes when she looked across
the distance between them. He saw confusion and shock.
He saw vulnerability and fear and sadness. And he saw
something else he couldn't quite identify.

Please, Lord, don't let it be disgust.

Sam hung his head. For the first time in over a decade,
he wished he wasn't a cop.

Captain Rogers arranged for additional men on the
property. Jacob and Rebecca bristled beneath the added
police presence. Jacob felt their agreement had been
breached. Sam was the only officer who was supposed
to be on his property, and Jacob didn't like the betrayal.
But at least they were trying to make the best of the situation. Rebecca invited the officers to join them for dinner.
Jacob treated his guests with the hospitality of the Amish.
The officers sensed the polite but distant ambience of
their hosts, and nobody at the table was happy right now.

Rebecca offered a platter of fried chicken to one of
the men. "Would you like some more, Officer Jenkins?"

The man smiled and raised a hand in a halting motion.
"No, ma'am. I couldn't eat one more bite. Everything was
delicious. Thank you for the invitation."

"A man needs to eat." Jacob glanced at his guest. "I
wouldn't want you to go away hungry."

The officer hid his chuckle in a napkin. Jacob did little
to hide how much he hoped the officers would be getting
ready to leave.

Both men stood up. "Thank you again for your hospitality. We'll be sitting outside in our squad cars if you need us. Just call."

The other man, Officer Muldoon, gave a curt nod in agreement with that statement and reached out to grab a chicken leg off the platter. "I'm gonna save this piece for later, if you don't mind." He raised it in the air as he backed toward the door. "I can't remember ever eating chicken so good."

"Will you be staying all night?" Jacob scowled at the men.

"Yes, sir. Our replacements will be here first thing in the morning."

"You can't sit in the car all night." Jacob's gruff tone caught everyone's attention. He placed his napkin on the table and rose. "*Kumm,* I will make a place for you in the barn. I have an oil burner. It will be warm."

"Thank you, sir. That would be much appreciated." They stood and followed Jacob out to the barn.

When the men left, the silence around the kitchen table became stifling. Sam glanced back and forth between Rebecca and Sarah. When neither woman spoke, he turned his attention to his meal. Although the aroma of fried chicken mingled in the air with the scent of cinnamon atop baked apples, Sam found no enjoyment in the dinner. It was simply fuel that his body needed. When he was finished, he thanked them and walked out of the room.

He grabbed a hurricane lamp and stepped out on the porch. Placing the lamp on the table, he sat down in one of the rockers and stared into the darkness.

Waves of pain washed over him as memories of days past entwined with the emotions of today's events. Pieces of buggy scattered and strewn in multiple directions. The sound of screams in the stillness of the night. A frightened whinny of a horse. A racing, reckless driver making stupid, irresponsible, dangerous choices. The sight of blood and lifeless bodies crumpled beneath wreckage as he scrambled through the carnage, begging and praying for survivors, only to find none.

His breath came in short, shallow gasps. Faces, sounds and sights raced through his mind.

He hadn't allowed himself to go to this deep, dark place for more than a decade. But here it was again. As though it had just happened, the pain fresh and intense.

He couldn't take it anymore. He bowed his head, cupped his face in his hands and sobbed.

Sarah helped Rebecca clear the table. She washed the dishes while Rebecca dried and put them away. Rebecca tried to maintain idle chatter, and when she realized Sarah was in no mood to talk—not about what to make for dinner tomorrow or even about how well Nathan's wife was recovering from her injury, and definitely not about the horrible events of the day—she finished her chores in silence.

Sarah couldn't think of anything but the day's events and the haunted look she saw in Samuel's eyes every time he looked at her. What had she done wrong? She knew she shouldn't have tried to stop him from loading his gun. He was a police officer, and that was a huge component of his job. But had that been enough to cause the anger and pain she saw in his eyes?

Still, she couldn't shake the way he had looked at her. Something was terribly wrong.

Once the chores were complete, Rebecca shooed Sarah into the living room. She told her to go sit in front of the fire. She'd make them a kettle of tea as soon as she was finished washing the floor.

Sarah left the kitchen but she didn't sit by the fire. Instead, she donned her sweater and slipped outside to find Samuel. She didn't have to go far. As soon as she stepped outside, she saw him sitting on the far end of the porch. He was hunched over, his face covered with his hands. She couldn't be sure, but from the muffled sounds she heard and the shaking of his shoulders, she thought he might be crying.

"Samuel?" She hurried to his side and placed a comforting hand on his back.

Sam startled at her touch. He jumped up from the rocker, dragged his forearm over his face and turned away.

"What are you doing out here? You should be resting."

She heard the catch in his voice, witnessed the effort it took him to regain control. She waited for a moment before speaking. "Can I help?"

He drew in a deep breath. Slowly, he turned to face her. "I'm sorry. I lost control for a moment, but I'm okay now. Truly, Sarah, go inside and go to bed. You need to rest, if not for yourself, then at least for your *boppli*."

He stayed in the shadows, and she couldn't see his face.

"Are you upset with me? I'm sorry I tried to stop you…"

"This has nothing to do with you, Sarah. Now please, go inside."

She stepped closer. So close they were both swallowed in the shadows cast by the hurricane lamp. She touched his arm. "Talk to me, Samuel. Tell me what torments you so."

For a moment, she didn't think he was going to answer her. When he did, his voice was gruff and harsh.

"It happened a long time ago. More than ten years now. Today stirred up those memories." He made a gruff sound. "Like I told you before, Sarah, memories are not always good things to have."

"Talk to me." She ran her hand down his arm and clutched his hand. "You have been such a good friend to me. Let me be a friend to you." She moved closer still, watching the kerosene light play across his features. "Tell me of this thing that troubles your soul."

He stepped into the light, and she was taken aback by the terrible pain she saw in his eyes. His expression reflected his indecision about whether he was going to talk to her about it. When he finally spoke, his words tumbled out with the force of a breaking dam.

Sarah never removed her hand from his. She smiled gently, encouragingly, and listened—until she thought her heart would break under the weight of his words.

"I was seventeen when I experienced the worst day of my life. Thanks to *rumspringe,* most of the restrictions my *daed* had enforced in my life were lifted. He turned a blind eye to the radio I'd sneak into the buggy when I'd take it to town. He'd pretend he didn't hear when I'd play music in my room and sing at the top of my lungs. When I'd had a few sips of beer that one of my *Englisch* friends had given me, I knew he smelled the alcohol on my breath. He scowled, his expression telling me he didn't approve, but he kept silent."

Sam turned his face away and stared into the darkness, but not before Sarah saw a tear trace its way down his cheek.

"But the one thing he wouldn't budge on was my curfew."

Sarah remained still, afraid to move, even breathe. She felt as if she was standing on the edge of a deep, dark crevice, and knew that whatever Sam was about to tell her had been buried for a very long time and had cut deep.

"I disobeyed the curfew. I didn't want to lose face with my friends. I was afraid they might taunt me for running home to Daed." He looked at her, and the pain she saw in his eyes seared her soul. "Friends? I can't even tell you the name of one of those boys today. Yet on that night they were more important to me than my father...or his rules."

Her eyes filled with tears. She wasn't even sure why. She just knew Sam was suffering, and there was nothing she could do to help him—except stay strong and silent and listen as he spoke about this thing, maybe for the very first time.

Sam's voice seemed wooden, his tone flat, empty. He stared off into the darkness. He might be standing here on the porch in front of her, but his spirit was gone—to another place, another time.

"It was dusk. Dark enough to trigger the streetlamps along the main street in town, but still light enough to recognize my father's buggy. I can still remember seeing him snap the reins when he saw me standing outside the local general store with my friends. Our horse fell into a trot, and the buggy headed in my direction.

"Some of my friends recognized my father's buggy, too. A few of the *Englisch* teens we were with had been drinking. They thought it was funny that my *daed* was out looking for me. They teased me, taunted me. When I didn't respond, they decided it might be more fun to taunt my father. They jumped in their car, revved their engines and drove down the street toward him."

Sarah's heart seized. She relived today's sound of an engine revving and the fear of watching a car swoop past their buggy. Her pulse pounded in her ears with fear as she remembered how hard Sam had fought to control the panicked horse. Suddenly present and past converged, and Sarah understood Sam's pain.

Today's incident had opened a portal into Sam's past, and everything he'd experienced came flooding back. She wanted to silence him. She wanted to pull him away from what she knew would be ugly, hurtful memories.

But it was too late. Sam was already standing in front of that general store, watching a car full of drunken teens descend upon his father.

"I didn't even know those boys. They were friends of a friend. Mere acquaintances. Older than me and the boys I was with." Sam rubbed his hand over his face. "They'd been drinking, and it affected their driving. They didn't mean to hit him. They thought it would be fun to scare him a little. But they were driving too fast and they lost control...."

Sam's words faded away, but it didn't matter. Sarah was with him now, standing beside the teenage Sam as he apprehensively watched his father approach, feeling the panic when he saw the car driving too fast and too close to the buggy. She held her breath and tightened her hold on his hand. She needed him to tell her the rest—and simultaneously wished he wouldn't.

"My father wasn't the only passenger in the buggy that night. My *maam* was with him. I didn't know it at first. I didn't know until after the buggy shattered into a million pieces, and I found their bodies in the rubble."

Sam looked at her. Flickers of lamplight danced across his face, but not even the shadows of the night could hide his tortured expression. "My mother was dead when I reached her. God was merciful. She died upon impact and didn't linger or suffer. My *daed*...his back was broken, his legs twisted at an odd angle beneath him, his breathing shallow and difficult. I remember he stayed awake and alert for a long time. Long enough for the police to arrive. Long enough for the paramedics to confirm my mother was dead.

"He held tight to my hand, and he kept saying the same words over and over again. I heard the words but they didn't really register...not then...not for years to come."

Sam drew his hand out of her grasp and ran his index finger softly down her cheek. His voice fell into a whisper. "My *daed* kept saying, 'I love you, son. Do not blame yourself. It was an accident.'" Sam's eyes glistened with fresh tears. "Isn't that the Amish way? To forgive the person who sinned against you?"

Sam stared off into space for several minutes before he spoke again, but when he did his words carried the pain and guilt of a young, frightened teenage boy who'd been unable to face his past.

"How could he do that, Sarah? Forgive? I killed my own family. Even God will never be able to forgive me."

FOURTEEN

"Hush, Samuel, don't say such a thing." Sarah wrapped her arms around him and pulled him close. "God knows our hearts. He can forgive us anything if we ask." She released her hold and cupped his face with her hands. "It is a terrible thing that happened that night. Terrible. But I agree with your father. It wasn't your fault."

"I broke curfew."

"*Ya,* just like hundreds of other teenagers trying to find their own way in this world. That's all you did."

"If I hadn't broken curfew, my parents would not have been in that buggy looking for me."

Sarah smiled tenderly at him. "Ah, Samuel, that is the hurt child inside of you speaking now. The man who stands in front of me knows that we do not have control over other people. Everyone made their own choices that evening. Your *dat* to search for you. Your *maam* to go with him. Those boys to drink and then drive recklessly."

She let her fingers trace a path down his cheek. "It would be prideful and foolish to think that we have power over other people, over life. Only God can claim that right, *ya?*"

"God?" Samuel scoffed. "Where was God that night? He allowed it. How could He permit such a terrible thing?"

"It is not our place to question God's plan. We do not know why He allows these things or how they affect His plan for our lives." The gentleness in Sarah's voice soothed him. "God never promised us that bad things wouldn't happen, Samuel. Just the opposite. The Bible tells us we will suffer many trials in this life. We only know He promises to be at our side to help us through when bad things do happen, and that somehow, in time, He makes all things work out for good."

"How is watching the murder of my parents a good thing? What good came of their deaths?"

Sarah folded her hands in front of her and smiled softly into his face. "I don't know. No more than I understand why Peter was killed or why my memory was erased. I don't understand why my neighbors are being punished because I am still alive. And, *ya,* I know how guilt can creep up on you and make you think that everything is your fault. But aren't you the one who told me everything that is happening now is not my fault? Did I shoot my husband? Terrorize the children in the school? Burn down my neighbors' barns?"

"No, of course not."

Sarah's smiled widened. "You're right. I am not responsible." She waited a heartbeat to allow her logic to penetrate his pain. "And you are not responsible for the tragedy that befell your family."

"You make it sound so easy."

"Easy? *Nee.* Suffering through trials is never easy. Simple? *Ya.* Put your faith in God, Samuel. Trust Him to run the world. He's been doing it for a very long time."

"How did you ever get to be so smart?"

"I don't know. I can't remember."

Sam laughed at her attempt at a joke, and Sarah joined in. When the moment passed, he drew her close. "Thank you." He wrapped one of the ties of her *kapp* around his finger. "I haven't spoken to anyone about that night. I thought I had dealt with it and buried it long ago. But today…I found myself reliving everything."

Sarah smiled up at him. "I'm glad I could be here for you."

His expression sobered. "I've never had anyone be there for me." He drew her close. His lips hovered inches above hers.

Sarah's pulse raced like birds taking flight, and a delightful shiver danced along her spine. She held her breath in anticipation. She didn't need to wait long.

When Sam lowered his head toward hers, he ignited feelings inside that she could no longer deny. She loved the feel of his breath as it whispered across her skin. She loved the softness and taste of his mouth as he claimed hers in a tender kiss. She loved the warmth and strength of his arms wrapped around her, holding her close, close enough that when she slid her hand along his shirt, she could feel the beating of his heart against her palm. She loved—

A bright light shone in their faces. Instinctively, they broke apart. Sarah raised a hand to shield her eyes.

"Um, sorry. I saw Mrs. Lapp come out onto the porch." The officer lowered his flashlight. "I didn't see you, Detective King. I thought she was alone, and when she disappeared into the shadows… Well, um, I thought I should check and make sure she was okay."

Even in the dim light from the kerosene lamp, Sarah could see a deep red flush on Sam's neck.

"You did the right thing, Officer." Sam stepped forward. "But, as you can see, Mrs. Lapp is unharmed."

The officer glanced back and forth between them. "Well, okay then." He gestured with his flashlight over his shoulder. "I'll just head back to the barn." He took a few more steps away. "And please thank Jacob for us again, Mrs. Lapp. The spring nights are still pretty cool, and that heater made it real comfortable in there."

Sarah watched him walk back to the barn. When he disappeared, she chanced a demure glance toward Sam. Suddenly, she felt awkward and unsure of herself—of them. What had really happened between them tonight? Had it been a simple kiss? An expression of gratitude when his emotions were running high? Or could it be something more? Could he be drawn to her as powerfully as she was to him? Could their friendship be turning into something deeper, something lasting, something that gave her hope for their future?

But she didn't find the answers she sought. His expression was inscrutable. There was no lingering sign of the tears he'd shed for his family. No warmth or tenderness directed to her after their kiss.

"You should go back inside, Sarah. It's not safe for you to be out here at night." His dismissive tone pierced her heart. It was like he could reach inside his mind and flip a switch from being a warm, tender, attentive man—*flip*—to a hard, cold, professional cop. A slow, seething anger surfaced inside.

"Not safe? From whom, Samuel? The man trying to kill me?" She stared hard at him. "Or you?"

She walked away and thought her heart might break because he didn't ask her to stay.

The wedding ceremony of Josiah and Anna had been simple but beautiful. Each time the bride smiled demurely at her groom, or the groom beamed his smile over the congregation, everyone could see how much in love the two of these young people were. At the conclusion of the ceremony, the women gathered to set up the food for the reception. The men moved the benches apart and squeezed as many tables as possible into the small space.

While setting plates and utensils on the tables, Sarah noticed Sam walk across the yard toward the barn. She smiled and greeted people as they inquired of her health and took their seats at the tables. She helped Rebecca carry out the hot casseroles and fresh bread. But her mind was elsewhere. She wondered why Sam had left the reception and what he was doing in the barn.

Sarah could barely squeeze through the cramped spaces between tables. Normally, Jacob would have erected a tent for the reception outside, but the heavy rainstorm from the other night had left puddles of mud and downed tree branches in its wake and changed those plans. Instead, the living room furniture had been pushed to the walls, and smaller chairs stored in bedrooms and outdoor tables and benches were overflowing through the great room, into the kitchen. One even rested at the entrance to a hall.

You'd think the cramped space would have put a damper on the wedding plans and upset the bride and groom, but it seemed to have a totally opposite effect. Everyone laughed and talked and rubbed elbows and laughed some more like one big happy family gathered for a holiday meal.

Then Sarah realized that that was exactly what this small community was—one large happy family. She smiled at the thought, and then gave a wistful sigh. She wondered if she would ever get her memory back. Even though everyone had been kind and helpful, she had no memory of them, no relationships with them, and she couldn't help but continue to feel like an outsider, always watching and never truly belonging.

She was making her third trip from the kitchen into

the great room when she glanced out the window and saw Sam. Now she understood why he'd left the group and gone to the barn. A smile tugged at her lips.

Sam waited while the groom pulled his wagon up to the barn entrance, and then jumped out and circled around the back to help. He removed the protective sheet he'd put on top of the table.

Josiah moved a hand lightly over the waxed-to-perfection table. "*Danki,* Samuel. You honored Peter's memory with this fine work."

Sam, embarrassed by the rare compliment, acknowledged it with a curt nod. "I hope Anna is pleased."

"Ah, how could she not be?" He stepped back, hands on hips, and studied the table. "It is a fine piece of furniture, is it not? Simple and plain, but sturdy and attractive too, *ya?*" He helped Sam cover the table, and then the two men lifted it into the back of the wagon. "This table will serve us well, Samuel. As our family grows, God willing, it will be the focal point of our home for prayers, meals, conversations. *Ya,* this is a good table."

They shook hands, and then both men headed back to the reception in the house.

Sam couldn't stop thinking about the table and the words Henry had spoken. It was true. The table was sturdy, well built and would service the family for years to come.

Peter had been the carpenter. He'd carved the wood lovingly with his own hands, building a piece of furniture that would withstand a baby banging a cup against it, support children doing their homework, bring a family together with hands joined and heads bent for prayer.

Sam wondered if Peter had thought about his own family when making the table. Jacob had told him that Peter was planning to start building his own house on the property in the spring—a place he was certain God would bless with the laughter and love of many children. Sarah and Peter had endured the emotional pain of two miscarriages. Sadness tugged at Sam's heart because Peter hadn't seen that prayer answered.

Sam was glad he could finish the gift that Peter had made for his newlywed friends. But now there was one more thing he could do in honor of the man's memory. He could find the man who had taken his life and threatened to end the life of his wife and unborn child. This is why he'd left his Amish ties so many years ago. To protect those unable to protect themselves. And with God's help, he would.

"Hurry, *kumm,* you are letting all the cold air into the house." Sarah laughed, braced the door open with her hands and ushered Sam into the house. "Josiah moved as quickly as a jackrabbit to get inside. You have been poking along like a turtle, and all the while I'm holding this door open for you."

Sam hung his hat on a peg by the door. "Do you know the rest of that story, Sarah? I believe it was the turtle who won the race."

Sarah's eyes widened with bewilderment. "What nonsense are you saying? When did you ever see a jackrabbit and a turtle race each other?"

Sam threw his head back and laughed. "Never mind. Go stand by the fire and warm yourself."

Sarah's smile was all he needed to feel warm. He watched her weave in and out between the tables, stopping for a quick word and always sharing a smile with many of the folks who spoke to her on her way. When she reached the fire, she shot him a quick look and then rubbed her hands together near the open flame.

"She looks happy today, *ya?*"

Sam had been so absorbed in watching Sarah that he hadn't heard Rebecca approach, and the sound of her voice startled him.

"Hello, Rebecca. Yes, she looks very happy today. It must be Josiah and Anna's wedding. The festivities seem to have lifted everyone's spirits."

"Not everyone's spirits were lifted today. Some of our hearts are still heavily burdened with loss." Her eyes glistened. "Let me ask you, Samuel. This man—the one who kills our loved ones, who burns our neighbors' barns…" Rebecca's voice choked as tears threatened to fall, but she took a deep breath and held them at bay. "How much longer do you think it will be before you find this man?"

"Soon, Rebecca." He hurried to reassure her and ease her pain. "He is getting careless and sloppy. He is out of his element now, in the country, not his familiar city setting, having to work quickly without help and not having the luxury of time to plot and double-check and plan. He is getting careless and frustrated and desperate. I believe it will be very soon when he will make a mistake that he will not be able to fix. Then we'll get him."

Rebecca considered his words and nodded. "*Gut.* Sarah needs this to be over. We all do."

Sam glanced in Sarah's direction and smiled. "Meanwhile, she is getting stronger and healthier each day."

Rebecca nodded. "*Ya,* that is true. Because she is home now, where she belongs—with her family and her community surrounding her, loving her, supporting her."

Sam straightened and tried not to bristle at the poorly veiled meaning behind her words.

Rebecca folded her hands in front of her and spoke just loud enough for him to hear. "I see the way you look at her, Samuel. More importantly, I see the way she looks at you."

He opened his mouth to protest, but Rebecca raised a hand in a silencing motion. "It is natural for her to have feelings for you. You are a *gut* man, strong, kind, protective. She feels vulnerable and afraid, and she has no memories of the man she loved…of the man whose child she carries…so she turns to you. I understand."

Sam didn't want to have this conversation, didn't want to hear what he knew Rebecca was about to say, but he remained silent and showed her respect by listening.

"You must be the strong one, Samuel. You must be the man whom all of us have come to know and respect. You must find this man—and I believe with God's help, you will—and then you must leave. Quickly. To ease her pain at seeing you go. We will take care of her when you are gone. After all, we are her family."

Rebecca locked her gaze with his. Sam almost had to look away from the pleading look in her eyes. "I have loved her as my own daughter since she was a small child on a neighboring farm. Often, she would come to our farm to play. I watched her grow into a beautiful young woman. I was so happy when Peter fell in love with her and asked her to be his wife."

She paused and stared off into space, reliving those distant memories. When she turned her attention back to him, she wore her pain like a heavy shawl.

"She carries my grandchild, the only part of Peter that I have left. Sarah's world is with us, and your world—" She shrugged her shoulders. "You made your choice many years ago, *ya?*"

Pain ripped through his heart as physically as if she had struck him with a dagger. But she was right. He had no intention of returning to the Amish community—and they would shun Sarah if he tried to take her with him.

"Be a *gut* man, Samuel. Be strong. Protect her from the evil of your world."

Anger bubbled beneath the surface and raced through his body. "Do you want what is best for Sarah, or what is best for you? Have you discussed this with her? Would she leave with me if I asked her to go?"

Rebecca sighed deeply. "No, Samuel. We did not speak of such things." Her gaze wandered to the other side of the room. Both of them watched Sarah as she teased and played with some children at a nearby table. Her laughter floated through the air like the tinkling of wind chimes and hovered over the rumble of conversations at the tables.

Rebecca turned her attention back to him. "I am not too old to remember what it feels like to give my heart to a man. When Sarah looks at you, I see it in her eyes. I think she has already given her heart. I think maybe she would go with you if you asked."

Rebecca stepped closer. "But just because someone *can* do something, Samuel, does not mean they *should* do it. Sometimes the wrong decision brings only heartache and pain. Be a *gut* man. Help Sarah make the right decision. You may not like my words, but you know my words are true. Sarah belongs here with her people, not in your world of evil and killing and pain."

She patted his hand like a mother who had just scolded her child, but wanted to assure the boy that he was not bad, just his actions.

He hadn't felt that motherly admonition for many years, and it was just that action that made him face the truth. She was right. He had to leave—soon—and if he loved Sarah, then he would be leaving alone.

Overcome with emotion, he grabbed his hat, donned his coat and stepped outside. He checked in with the other two officers watching the house, told them he would be out of contact for a bit and to keep a sharp eye on Sarah.

With bent head and heavy heart, he walked away.

The man's teeth chattered, and he salted the air with a string of curses. He should be home. He envisioned himself standing before a roaring fire with a snifter of brandy in his hand as he looked through the wall of glass to the ocean below. That's where he belonged.

Not here, perched in a tree, hidden by leaves and clinging to branches so he wouldn't fall to his death.

He cursed John Zook. Why had he ever allowed the man to join his team? What a colossal mistake that had been, and he wasn't a man who made many mistakes.

Who would have ever believed that stupid Amish lout would find the backbone to steal his diamonds? Steal! From him!

He should have cut his losses and called an end to this long ago. After all, he certainly didn't need the money. His expertise at ridding the rich of their wealth had served him well over the years. A smile bowed his lips when he pictured some of the art and fine gems in his collection.

No, it was not the loss of the diamonds. Money could always be replaced. And what did it matter, since none of it had been his in the first place?

It was the betrayal he couldn't forgive.

No one betrayed him and lived.

So he'd followed Zook and punished him appropriately. He hadn't anticipated the resulting mess. The Amish husband rushing to his wife's defense. The woman surviving—twice—but unable to remember. Yet.

He definitely had a mess on his hands, and he didn't like messes.

But it would soon be over.

If he killed the woman, then none of the others would dare come forward. He'd read that the Amish were big on forgiveness. They often didn't prosecute offenders and rarely testified in courts. Yep, kill the woman and the others would be so afraid for their children—and themselves—that he would feel safe to return home, where he belonged. He couldn't bear being away for even one more night.

Today it would end.

He glanced at the sky. The sun would be setting shortly. The party at the Lapp residence would soon be over. He'd have to act fast. He'd thought it over and decided it would be easier to strike when hundreds of people milled about the place rather than try to isolate her when she was on her own.

He wasn't worried about the cops. Oh, they kept watch over her, sure. But they could be easily distracted. They weren't as invested in her well-being as that one who'd followed her here from the hospital. There was probably something going on between the two of them. But he didn't care. He hoped the guy got what he wanted from his lady friend because their little romance was coming to an end real quick.

He lifted binoculars to his eyes for another surveillance of the party and couldn't believe his good fortune. That cop—the undercover one who thought he could fool him by dressing Amish—was leaving.

He adjusted the lens and took a second look. He watched him consult with the other two cops and then walk off. He watched his hurried gait, his bent head, his stooped shoulders.

Uh-oh. Something had happened. A love spat, maybe? This guy didn't look happy, and he definitely didn't look like he was coming back .

It was time. He smiled in anticipation. Soon this would

be over. He would be home and safe. He could almost taste the brandy on his lips.

With agile movements, he lowered himself to the ground. He had to move fast—and it had to be now.

FIFTEEN

"William, you forgot your sweater." Sarah stood in the doorway, waving them in front of her. The boy rushed back, took the sweater from her with a hurried *"Danki,"* and ran off to join the mass of children playing in the yard.

Benjamin came up beside her in the doorway. *"Danki,* Sarah. I worry about that boy. His head is always in the clouds."

"He is young still, Benjamin. He will settle down soon enough."

Benjamin frowned. "Sometimes he seems so distracted, I worry he can't walk a straight line across the yard." Benjamin shook his head. "Always getting into trouble, that one. Not bad behavior. Just foolish behavior from not thinking things through."

"How old is he now? Seven? Eight?"

"Seven. Old enough to stop all that daydreaming."

"Who knows? Maybe William will use his creativity to be a great writer or painter."

Benjamin frowned. "Sarah, you should know by now that the Amish do not take great stock in those foolish things. I will be happy if he is a great farmer."

Sarah chuckled. "Ah, but Benjamin, think about it. The good Lord created all of us. Each one of us is the same, yet different. It is those differences, those individual talents, that make us unique and special, *ya?*"

Before he could reply, both Benjamin and Sarah ducked as a baseball flew past their heads and crashed through the front window.

"Sorry, Daed. I was trying to throw the ball to you." William, wearing a worried expression, stood at the bottom of the steps looking up at them.

Benjamin frowned. "Throw it to me? Did you call my name? Did you let me know the ball was coming my way? Look what you've done to Bishop Lapp's window. Think what you could have done if you had hit me in the head!"

William hung his head. "I'm sorry, Daed. I will do chores for the bishop to help pay for the broken glass."

"That you will!" Benjamin looked at Sarah. "See what I mean? Now I must speak to Jacob about this." Sighing heavily, he reached down to retrieve his hat, which had fallen to the ground, plopped it on his head and went back inside.

"I didn't mean to hit the window," William said, his gaze trailing after his father.

"I know you didn't." Sarah lowered her voice to a whisper. "But next time you aim for your father, William, make sure he knows it is coming. Now go back and play." She shooed him away.

Sarah stepped back inside the house. Most of the adults were preparing for their trip home. The women finished washing dishes and wrapping up leftover food. The men carried the benches out to the wagon used to transport them from farm to farm for services, and then they collapsed and stored the long plastic picnic tables for future use.

"Anything I can do to help, Mrs. Lapp?"

Sarah glanced at Officer Muldoon. He looked too

young to be a cop. She bet his *maam* found it difficult to watch him don the uniform and walk out the door with a gun strapped to his side each day. Sarah placed a hand on her swelling belly and thanked God she would never have to carry that worry in her heart for her child. The worst that could happen to him or her was to be kicked by a horse or hurt by some farm equipment.

She'd found it difficult to see Samuel carry a gun. He hadn't liked it, but had complied with her wishes when she asked that the gun be put away for this occasion. There were so many women and children attending today's wedding. This was not a time or place for guns.

Sarah glanced around and then looked back at the officer. "Have you seen Detective King anywhere?"

"He left about an hour ago. He asked us to keep an eye on things."

"Left?" A frown twisted her lips. "Where did he go?"

"Don't know. Didn't ask. But you're in good hands, don't worry."

"I'm not worried, Officer Muldoon. I am sure you will do a good job."

Sarah smiled and then walked away.

How strange. Even in the hospital, Samuel had barely left her out of his sight. Since they came home from the hospital, he'd never been farther than the sound of her voice. So why would he suddenly leave without a word of his whereabouts to anyone? It seemed so unlike him.

Seeing the bride and groom preparing to leave, she hurried over to offer her congratulations and best wishes for their future together. En route, she said her goodbyes to several other families that were heading out. When she'd accomplished her task, she sat down in front of the fireplace to rest—and think.

She still couldn't understand Samuel's sudden disappearance. She knew he didn't owe her any explanation—but still. She thought back to the last time she'd seen him, and then remembered him standing by the front door speaking with Rebecca. Maybe he'd said something to her.

Sarah found Rebecca in the kitchen putting away the dishes. "Do you need any help?"

"*Danki,* child, but no. This is the last of it. Many hands made the work disappear fast." Rebecca sent a puzzled look her way. "Is everything all right? You look troubled."

"Everything's fine. I was just wondering if Samuel might have said something to you before he left. I saw him talking with you earlier, and I haven't seen him since."

Rebecca's cheeks flushed a bright red, and she averted her eyes. If Sarah didn't know better, she would have thought the woman felt guilty about something. But that certainly couldn't be the reason for the flush, could it?

"Rebecca?"

The older woman tucked pots into lower drawers on the stove, and then pretended to wash an already clean countertop.

"Do you know why Samuel left? Or where he went?" Sarah asked.

Rebecca turned and planted her hands on her hips. "I think you pay that young man much too much attention. We both know that his job brought him here, and when the job is done he will leave. It is best you remember that and go about your business."

Stunned by her harsh tone, Sarah simply nodded and stepped away. She'd never heard Rebecca utter a stern word before, and it shocked her. Of course, she couldn't remember if there had been any harsh words spoken between them in the past. She could only base her opinion on her experience with the woman now.

Maybe the stress of the past month, along with everything that happened since Sarah had come home, was catching up with Rebecca. Yes, that must be it. The woman was tired and still grieving. A bit out of sorts. Anyone would be. She'd have to be a little kinder, a little quicker to offer help.

But still…

Something didn't feel right. Sarah thought Rebecca knew much more than she was saying.

Wrapping a shawl around her shoulders, Sarah stepped onto the front porch. Maybe a little walk would do her good, make her feel less restless. She told herself that she was just getting some exercise. She would not allow herself to believe she was looking for Samuel.

"Going somewhere, Mrs. Lapp?"

"Officer Muldoon, please call me Sarah. I have trouble remembering to answer to Mrs. Lapp."

"Yes, ma'am."

Sarah smiled. "And please don't call me ma'am. In our language, that means mother." She squelched a giggle at the bashful and embarrassed look he sent her way.

"Yes, ma'am…uh, Sarah." He looked around and then asked, "Are you walking alone? Would you like me to accompany you?"

"No, that won't be necessary. I'm not venturing far. I just feel the need to stretch my legs."

As they spoke, Officer Jenkins appeared. "Everything okay here?"

Sarah laughed. "How could it not be with so many attentive gentlemen watching over me?" She folded her hands in front of her. "I just wanted to stretch my legs. You can both sit on the porch. I promise I won't leave your sight. I just want some time alone with my thoughts."

"Seems to be a lot of that going around lately."

Sarah raised an eyebrow in question.

"Detective King told me the same thing not so long ago." Jenkins nodded toward the porch. "We'll wait over there. But please don't leave the yard."

Sarah acknowledged his words with a nod and continued her walk.

Samuel needed time alone with his thoughts?

Once again the niggling feeling that Rebecca knew more than she was saying returned. She'd only strolled a few yards when the ground shook beneath Sarah's feet, and the sound of an explosion deafened her.

Children who had still been playing in the yard raced for the safety of their parents' arms. Screams rent the air. Men's voices of alarm and concern added to the cacophony. The police officers scrambled off the porch. Jenkins ran to their vehicle. Muldoon hurried to her side.

Jenkins shouted to Muldoon. "Get her back in the house, and don't let her come out until we know what's going on!" His voice brooked no argument. Muldoon nodded.

Sarah watched the patrol car, lights flashing, speed down the lane.

"C'mon, Mrs….Sarah, let's get you inside."

They were hurrying toward the house when Jacob rushed past. Sarah reached out to stop him. "What's happened?"

"I don't know." Jacob pointed in the distance to a large plume of black smoke. "There's been some kind of explosion in the west end of my cornfield. But nothing is there to cause such a thing. Stay calm. It will be all right. We will follow the police officers and find out what is happening. Stay inside with the rest of the women." Before Sarah could respond, he hurried to a buggy hitched at the rail, climbed aboard and snapped the reins, leading the horse in the direction of the smoke.

When they reached the bottom step of the porch, Officer Muldoon released her arm. "Go inside, Sarah. I'm going to make a fast check of the perimeter of the house and the barn, and then I'll be right in."

Before she could reply, he disappeared around the corner of the house.

Sam leaned against a bale of hay and glanced toward the house. The loft of a barn had been his favorite spot as a child to find a quiet, private place to be with his thoughts, and he found it worked for him as an adult, too. The slow, steaming anger he had felt toward Rebecca at her blatant request for him to leave slowly dissipated.

She was right. How could he be angry with someone who spoke the truth? So he cooled down and gave her words some more thought. It didn't take long for him to realize that he'd never really been angry with Rebecca. He was angry with himself.

What had he been thinking? He knew better than to mix his professional life with his personal life. That was rule number two in undercover work. Rule number one was to stay alive at all costs. He should never have allowed himself to get too close to Sarah, to care about her. He shouldn't have—but he did.

He rubbed a hand over his face. He couldn't deny it anymore. It had begun as sympathy for a wounded widow, then admiration for her spirit and determination. It had progressed to appreciation of her gentle nature and enjoyment of her sense of humor until, without knowing exactly where or when, he'd fallen in love with her. When he looked into her eyes, he could see that she had fallen in love with him, too. That was the worst part.

The fact that he had never intended to hurt her didn't mean much when he knew that he would. There was no future for them. He couldn't return to the Amish way of life. He'd left it more than a decade before, and although he still retained a love for the Amish people, it was no longer his world.

And Sarah…

Even though she had no memory of this life, she still had strong, loving ties. What was he supposed to do? Take her away from the people who loved her? Ask her to sit in his small apartment all alone because he was off for days, weeks, sometimes even months on undercover jobs? What kind of life would that be for her? For her child?

No. Rebecca was right. If he loved her—and he did—then he needed to leave as quickly as possible, just as soon as this was over. One broken heart was enough. Best it be his.

Satisfied that he was making the right decision, he began to crawl out from behind the bale of hay. He intended to climb down the ladder, relieve the other two officers and have a heart-to-heart talk with Sarah.

The sound of an explosion froze him in place.

He scrambled toward the ladder, but stopped when he saw a stranger enter the barn. It was the stealth of the man's movements, the way he kept looking over his shoulder, that made Sam pause.

Mary and William Miller were playing on the barn floor below.

Sam couldn't believe what he was seeing, and he had to force himself not to move when the man grabbed Mary roughly by the arm and dragged her toward the far end of the barn. The intruder stood just below him, which made it difficult for Sam to get a clear view of what he was doing without exposing his presence and putting Mary at greater risk.

Sam's brain raced a million miles an hour. Who was

this man dressed in Amish clothing? He'd seen him before. It definitely wasn't Benjamin. As strict as Benjamin was, he loved his children and would never treat them in such a rough, unkind way. Sam was just about to speak up and reveal his presence when recognition slammed into him with the force of a semi truck.

This was the man he'd fought in Sarah's hospital room. Even though it had been dark and he'd only seen him for a moment, he was sure it was the same man.

This was their killer.

As he watched in horror, trying to formulate a plan, William ran to Mary's defense. Like a charging bull, he pushed against the man, then yelped like an injured puppy and pulled his hand back. The man had sliced the palm of William's hand with a knife.

Fury seethed within him. It took every ounce of strength he had to stay where he was. But he'd seen the silver glint of a blade pressed firmly against Mary's throat. Sam knew this man wouldn't hesitate to use the weapon if he were startled or if he discovered his presence.

Sam dared to lean forward. He took another glance at the situation. His heart melted when he saw tears streaming down Mary's cheeks. He hoped she'd do what she was told and remain still. This particular intruder had no conscience. He wouldn't care in the least that the life he ended would be that of an innocent child.

As quietly as possible, Sam crept back into the shadows. He needed to signal for help. He moved to the loft door to see if he could spot the other officers. He didn't catch sight of either one of them. But what he did see turned his blood to ice.

Sarah had reached the top porch step when she thought she heard someone calling her name and turned around. William stood at the base of the steps, looking up at her.

"William?" Sarah's heart clenched. The boy's face was as white as the sheets on the line, and his entire body trembled. She hurried down the steps, crouched in front of him and placed a comforting hand on his shoulder. "What's wrong?"

The little boy's lips trembled. He spoke in a whisper, and she had to lean closer to hear. "He…he told me to get you. He told me to bring you to the barn."

Sarah glanced toward the barn and then back to the boy, who was literally shaking in his boots. "Who told you, William? What man?"

"A bad man, Sarah. A very bad man." William's eyes were wider than she thought his little face could hold.

"Okay, honey. Let me get Officer Muldoon, and we'll come into the barn."

As Sarah started to rise, the boy grabbed her arm with both his hands. "No! The man said nobody could come but you." Then the boy collapsed into her arms and began to cry.

"Shh, William, everything will be okay." She held the child against her, rubbing his back in comfort while searching the yard for help. Seconds ago there had been people everywhere. Since the explosion, there wasn't a person in sight. Sarah continued to pat William's shoulder. "Your parents are inside. Let's go talk with them."

"No!" William looked terrified. "We can't tell my parents. We can't tell anyone or he'll kill her. He told me so."

Sarah felt the blood in her body drain away. "Kill who? William, tell me everything, please, right now." She tried to remain calm and keep her voice controlled so the boy wouldn't panic. The strength seemed to drain out of her legs, and she didn't know how much longer she trusted them to hold her up.

"We were playing in the barn when a man ran in, grabbed Mary and pulled her into one of the horse stalls. He held her real tight so she couldn't run away. He told me to come and get you. He told me to make sure we didn't bring anyone else."

"We don't listen to bad men, William. Of course we are going to bring people with us to help Mary." Sarah placed one foot on the lower step, but William threw himself at her, almost as if he were trying to tackle her.

"Please, no." His eyes pleaded with her. "If you tell anyone, then he said he will cut her worse than he cut me." He held out his left hand.

Sarah took hold of his tiny hand. Her eyes could barely pull away from the sight of the thin red line slashed across the boy's palm.

"Dear Lord, help us. Why didn't you tell me that he'd hurt you?" For the first time, she noticed the stark droplets of red on the ground at the boy's feet. She quickly untied her apron and used it to tend to the boy's wound. She applied a steady pressure against his palm.

After a moment, she lifted the material and breathed a sigh of relief. The cut had been superficial and not deep. The bleeding stopped immediately. No permanent damage had been done. He wouldn't need stitches or even have a scar.

"Danki, Lord."

William couldn't hold back tears anymore, even though they both knew his father would find it a sign of weakness for a boy to cry. His breathing came in hiccups. "He…he is holding a knife against Mary's throat. She can't even try to run away, or he will cut her. Please. You have to help Mary."

Sarah hugged him close. When she released him, she held his forearms and stared hard into his eyes. "I am going to go into the barn and try to help Mary, but you must help me. Do you understand?"

The boy nodded.

"Good. You stay here. You count to ten very slowly. Then you run inside and tell your father everything. Counting to ten will give me time to get into the barn. After the bad man sees that I am alone, he won't be expecting anyone else. It will be safe for you to tell your father and let him bring people to help me." She gave William's shoulders a gentle shake. "This is important, William. Do you understand? Count to ten slowly, and then go inside and get help."

Although the boy nodded, she didn't like the dazed expression on his face. This was not a time for William to get distracted or daydream as he frequently did, but she didn't have a choice except to trust him. If this man had used a knife on William, she had no doubt that he'd use one on Mary, and she couldn't let that happen. She offered up a silent prayer that the boy would do as she'd requested, and she hurried to the barn.

Stopping right outside the entrance, she took a deep breath to steady the trembling that seized her body. She glanced over her shoulder. William stood right where she'd left him, his eyes riveted on her. She did her best to smile reassuringly. She nodded in his direction and then, slowly pushing the door open, stepped inside. Her breath caught in her throat the moment she spotted the stranger. He stood at the far end of the barn in the entrance to one of the stalls. The knife he held pressed against the little girl's throat was clearly visible.

"Don't cry, Mary. Everything is going to be all right. Try not to move, honey." Although the beat of her heart galloped like a wild stallion on stampede, Sarah kept her voice steady and her outward composure calm.

Please, God, be with this child. Please keep her as still as possible until William can bring help.

"Come in, Sarah. Shut the door behind you." The tenor of the intruder's voice rose and fell in a singsong rhythm. "I've been waiting for you."

SIXTEEN

Fear danced up and down Sarah's spine. "Please. Let her go." She took several steps toward the man. "She is just a child. She has nothing to do with any of this."

The man stepped out of the stall, dragging the girl with him. He sneered, and for a moment Sarah couldn't believe she was even looking at a human being. He seemed to have no heart, no compassion. She found herself looking into the eyes of pure evil.

"Where are my diamonds?" he demanded.

Sarah had to take several breaths before she was able to calmly answer. "I have never seen your diamonds. The police told me they found them on my body when they took me to the hospital. They must still have them."

"Police, huh. Figures." He yanked the child closer, and she whimpered with fear. "So what are you going to do to make it up to me, Sarah? What can you offer me in exchange for my diamonds…and for the life of this girl?"

Sarah's legs shook so badly that she felt they would dump her on the dirt floor at any moment. Her mind raced, but she couldn't come up with any plan of action that would ensure the girl's safety, and she knew there was little hope for her own. She prayed that William had done what she requested and that help would be racing through the open barn door at any moment. She moved closer so she could throw herself against the man and try to save Mary as soon as she heard help coming.

"Stop right there!"

The command in his voice froze her in place.

"Do you think I'm stupid? I can see exactly what you have in mind. It's written all over your face. You think you can wrestle this knife from me and save the child. I may even let you do it." He let out a maniacal laugh. "I'll even do one better. I'll give you a choice. I can slit this child's throat right now...or you can step forward so I can claim the life of the child you carry."

In horror, Sarah's hands flew to her belly, and for a moment she couldn't move, couldn't think.

"That's what I thought. So it will be the girl." Before he could move his hand across her throat, a small voice echoed in the barn.

"No! Let my sister go!" William had crept into the barn behind Sarah and now stepped out into the open, drew something from his pocket and, before anyone could blink, launched an object into the air.

It took only seconds for Sarah to realize that William had a slingshot in his hand, and his stone had hit its mark.

The stranger groaned and automatically lifted his right hand to his forehead, freeing the knife from Mary's neck. The girl dropped to the barn floor and scrambled away on all fours. Sarah and William raced forward to help her. At the same time, a large, dark object fell out of the loft and landed on top of the stranger.

"Help! Somebody help us. Help!" Sarah screamed at the top of her lungs as she pulled William and Mary toward the open barn door. It wasn't until they'd cleared the barn and were standing safely in the yard that Sarah sent the children racing to the house for help and dared to turn and look behind her to see what had fallen on the intruder.

Her eyes widened in horror. It wasn't a thing. It was Samuel. Both men were in the fight for their lives as they wrestled on the dirt floor of the barn.

Glancing over her shoulder, she saw the children burst into the house.

Sarah ran back into the barn, grabbed a pitchfork and hurried toward the men. She never had to wonder whether or not she'd be capable of piercing the man with it. She couldn't get a clear poke at him. His back would be toward her for a split second, then just as quickly it would be Sam's.

Sarah danced around the two men looking for an opportunity to help, but she needn't have worried. After a few well-aimed punches, Sam had the situation under control. He straddled the man, holding the stranger's hands behind his back.

"Sarah, place that pitchfork on the back of this man's neck."

Nausea rose in Sarah's throat.

"Do it. Now," Sam commanded.

It took a moment of supreme trust in Samuel, but Sarah did as he asked.

Sam grabbed the weapon from Sarah's hands. "I'm holding this pitchfork now, and I will not hesitate to use it on the likes of you. Understand?" He exerted a little more pressure, and the man stayed absolutely still. "Smart decision," Sam said. Then he glanced up at Sarah. "Find Officer Muldoon and get him out here. Then go and get my gun."

Sarah ran from the barn just as a half-dozen Amish men rushed past her into the barn. When she returned, the gun held at arm's length in front of her and hanging gingerly from her fingers, Sam looked like he was trying not to laugh at her. The Amish men, armed with sticks, baseball bats and a second pitchfork, had formed a circle around him and the intruder. They seemed to be doing their best to look threatening, but Sam knew that not one of them would connect a blow, and the entire scene was staged for support, not protection.

Sarah hurried forward, and he took the gun from her fingers. He loosed his hold on the pitchfork, ordered the other Amish men to step away and hauled the intruder to his feet.

Officer Muldoon stumbled into the barn. The back of his head and the shoulder of his jacket were coated with blood. Despite his injury, he moved forward, drew his weapon and stood next to Sam.

"I'm sorry, Detective King. I was checking the perimeter of the house when someone got me from behind."

"Meet the somebody who clocked you. You okay?"

"I will be."

"Good. Cuff him and get him out of here."

Sam supervised the cuffing and had started to walk with Muldoon to the car when Jenkins raced into the barn, assessing the situation in an instant. He stepped forward, replaced Sam's hold on the perp's arm and helped escort him to his patrol car.

Sam thanked the Amish men for their support and watched as they filed out behind the police officers. Sam smiled again.

Finally, he had a chance to focus his attention on Sarah. He clasped her forearms and felt the trembling beneath his fingers cease. Her eyes, filled with concern and caring, caught his gaze and melted him to the spot. His heart thundered in his chest. His pulse raced.

Before he could give it a moment's thought, he pulled her into his arms and kissed her. This kiss wasn't tender or tentative. All of the emotions he had tried to hide surfaced in an embrace of passion and fire and need.

And she kissed him back.

She fit in his arms as naturally as if she'd always belonged there. She threaded her fingers in his hair and wrapped her other arm tightly around his waist. She tasted of strawberries and coffee and tears.

It was a delicious, intoxicating kiss—and he wanted more. When he lifted his mouth, the flush of her skin and the brightness in her eyes made him smile.

"Are you all right?" he asked. "Did that man hurt you?"

"*Nee,* I am fine." She smiled so widely it barely fit her face. "Samuel, you saved us."

"I wish I could have done something sooner, but he had too tight a hold on Mary for me to take the chance. If it wasn't for William's bravery..." He directed the words to Benjamin who had just reentered the barn, closely followed by Jacob and the others. "That is a brave, fine boy you have."

Benjamin's voice croaked. "*Danki,* Samuel. William was very brave today, it's true."

Although the Amish try not to show favor, pride shone from Benjamin's eyes, and Sarah believed God would forgive this moment of transgression.

"Who was that man, Samuel?" Aaron Miller asked from the middle of the crowd.

"That is the man who shot Sarah and killed Peter. He is a career criminal who has made a lifetime of stealing art and fine gems to support his expensive lifestyle. He made fatal mistakes when he entered a world he was not familiar with. No one will have to worry about him again."

"What happens now, Samuel?" Jacob stepped forward. "What will they do with that man?"

"He will go on trial. Based on the evidence we have against him, he will spend the rest of his miserable life in a cell. He will never be a threat to you or your family again."

Jacob nodded. "*Danki,* Samuel."

"Don't thank me. Everyone worked together. The children, Sarah, yourselves. You graciously allowed the intrusion into your home and into your lives. But it's over now."

"Yes, it's over." Rebecca stepped out of the shadows and stood beside her husband.

Sam took one look at the expression on her face, and he knew that she had witnessed the kiss.

"We must say a prayer of thanksgiving to the Lord," Rebecca said. Her gaze locked with his. "God is good. Sarah is safe. The man has been captured. He will be punished in an *Englisch* court under *Englisch* law. And our lives can return to what they should be." Rebecca stared hard at him. "Isn't that so, Samuel?"

Sam's stomach clenched. His arms still ached with the feel of Sarah within them. His lips still tasted her lips. He knew what the woman expected of him. Now he had to ask himself if he was man enough to do it.

Sarah watched the exchange between Samuel and Rebecca. She heard the words. Nothing out of the ordinary had been said, but something unspoken hung in the air.

Seconds of silence stretched between them, and then Samuel nodded. "Yes, Rebecca. Now is the time for your lives to return to normal."

"*Gut.*" She stepped forward and hugged Sam. "You are a *gut* man, Samuel. God bless you."

Sarah wasn't sure what she had just witnessed, but a sense of dread overcame her.

Rebecca ushered the others out of the barn to regroup, check on the children and have a cup of coffee before their departure. Sarah had started to go with them when Sam's hand shot out and stopped her.

"Sarah..."

She stared into his eyes and almost had to look away from the pain she saw looking back at her.

Gently, he cradled her face with his hands.

"Sweet, sweet Sarah."

His eyes glistened, and for a brief moment she thought he might cry.

When the others were out of sight, he pulled her to him. He kissed her again—a passionate kiss, a desperate kiss—and suddenly Sarah knew. It was a goodbye kiss.

She lifted her eyes and searched his face, hoping she was wrong, but the shuttered look in his eyes told her she wasn't. Still, she tried to deny the inevitable. She offered him a tentative smile. "When you are finished with whatever you have to do for your job, you are welcome to join us for dinner. Rebecca is making a pot roast, and I still have some of your favorite apple pie left."

"Sarah..."

"If you can't make it back this evening, that's okay. We understand you have many things to do. You are welcome to join us tomorrow night."

He placed his hands on her waist and held her in place.

"It's over. My job here is done. It is time for me to go home."

Her breath seized in her throat, and her heart refused to beat. She had known this moment would come, but she'd hoped...she'd prayed...

"Your home could be here, Samuel. You are Amish. You could return to your roots, study, get baptized. Our community would welcome you."

"I am not Amish. I haven't been for more than a decade." He trailed a finger down her cheek. "You are a very special woman. A loving woman. Smart. Kind. Brave." Boldly but gently, Sam placed his hand on her stomach. "God knew what He was doing when he chose you to be the mother of this child."

She placed her hand on top of his and clasped his fingers. "Samuel…please, don't…"

"I will always cherish the moments you allowed me to share with you." He removed his hand. "We both knew this time would come, and now that time is here. I must return to my world—and you must stay in yours."

"But is this my world?" Sarah's eyes filled with tears. "I have no memories of this life. I have no memories of *any* life. As you told me yourself, I can be whoever I want to be. The future has not yet been written."

He smiled sadly. "You will have a wonderful future here with your family—raising your child and surrounded by the people who love you."

"What about who *I* love?" She challenged him with her eyes. "Don't my feelings matter?" She hesitated and then took the chance and spoke. "I…I don't remember Peter. You are the only man I know. You are the only man I…I…"

He placed a finger against her lips before she could finish.

"Shh. Think, Sarah. You love Rebecca. You love Jacob. And they and all the people in this community love you in return. They are your family. You belong here." He drew her into his arms and hugged her tightly. His breath was like a gentle breeze through her hair. "Go with God, Sarah. Be happy. It is best you do not dwell on everything that happened in this past month. Try to put it all behind you and move on."

"Is that what you truly want, Samuel? For me to forget you, too, as I have forgotten everything else?" She stared defiantly into his eyes, daring him to look away.

He released her. He tilted her chin up and kissed her on the forehead. His tenderness ripped at her heart. "In those quiet moments of the evening, when you sit on the porch and stare at the sky, I want you to know that the feelings we had for each other were real. The respect. The friendship. The warmth."

"The love?" Sarah could barely whisper the question.

He dropped his gaze from hers. "Our time together was special. Something to be cherished. A memory, Sarah. A memory that no one will ever be able to take away."

He placed a gentle kiss on her lips, and Sarah could have sworn she tasted the salt of his tears. When she opened her eyes, she stared at his back as he walked out of her life as suddenly as he had swooped in.

SEVENTEEN

"I wish you had stayed home," Rebecca scolded as she stepped down from the buggy and turned to help Sarah down as well. "Soon you will be delivering that wee one. These bumpy carriage rides cannot be helping."

Sarah grasped Rebecca's hand and used it to steady herself as she moved her cumbersome girth and stepped down. Her foot twisted, and she started to fall.

Rebecca gasped and reached out to try to grab her, but her hold was too weak to help.

Before Sarah hit the ground, two strong hands grabbed her from behind and righted her. When she regained her footing, she turned with a smile to thank the person who had helped her, but the words locked in her throat.

Tears welled in her eyes. She had truly believed she would never see him again. But here he was. Not an apparition or a dream, but a flesh-and-blood man standing mere inches away from her.

"Samuel?"

He shuffled his feet and stared at the ground. It was obvious he was as uncomfortable with their encounter as she was.

"What are you doing here?" She held her breath and waited for his answer.

"I quit my job in Philadelphia. I got a job here with the Lancaster Sheriff's Department." He dared a quick glance her way and shrugged. "I kept telling everyone I became a cop to protect the Amish community. Figured if I planned to really do that, then I belonged here with the Amish."

His sheepish grin tugged at her heart.

He was back. For good.

What did that mean? Did she dare hope?

"Are you telling me that you live here now…in Lancaster, I mean?"

"Yes." He tucked his thumbs into the utility belt on the waist of his police uniform.

Sarah's eyes couldn't get enough of him. He looked tall and dangerous and absolutely delightful. And he was back.

"I bought a place not far from town," he said. "The older couple who had owned it couldn't keep up with the repairs. I'm fixing it up little by little on weekends and any hours I have away from work."

"Are you talking about the Townsend farm?" Rebecca asked. She hid her shock at seeing him as well, but the tremor in her voice gave her away. "I'd heard they'd sold their property to a young investor and moved away."

Sam laughed. "I don't consider myself an investor. Don't know if I'd qualify as young these days, either. But yes, I bought the Townsend place."

The sound of his deep chuckle sent a wave of warmth through Sarah's veins.

He's back. Sam came back.

"The Townsend place…isn't that the farm down the hill from ours?" Sarah asked.

Sam locked his gaze with hers. "Yes."

Had he come back for her? And if he had…

Sarah glanced at Rebecca and saw the question and fear residing in the older woman's eyes.

Myriad emotions raced through her. Could she leave the Amish community knowing they would shun her? She'd never be able to continue her relationship with Rebecca and Jacob. Could she bear that? Would she be any happier in the *Englisch* world than she had been in the Amish one? Since her memory had never returned, how would she be able to answer the questions tumbling through her mind?

And then she knew.

It wasn't her mind that would answer those questions. It was her heart…and her heart belonged to Samuel.

She stared at him, waiting for him to say the words she longed to hear. She tried to understand his silence, searched for a hidden message in his eyes, an invitation, but she didn't see one. Her exhilaration and hope quickly faded.

"It was good seeing the two of you again. I expect we'll bump into one another now and again. Give Jacob my best."

He was getting ready to walk away…again.

Please, God, not again. Please.

"Well, you ladies have a nice afternoon."

Sarah couldn't believe it. He hadn't returned for her. He wasn't here to ask her to be his bride. She stared at his back in silence and wondered just how many times her heart could break before there wouldn't be any pieces left.

Walking away from Sarah for the second time was one of the hardest things he had ever had to do. He loved the woman. He'd always love the woman. And that's how he found the strength to leave.

She belonged with Rebecca and Jacob. She was close to term with her pregnancy, and the birth of this baby would seal her role within their family.

He knew he should have stayed in Philadelphia. What had he been thinking?

Sam hadn't been thinking. He'd been feeling. He knew he couldn't have a life with Sarah, but he couldn't live a life without her, either. So he satisfied himself with the occasional glimpse, the few idle words spoken on the street. And he prayed, something that hadn't come easily to him but was now part of his daily life. He prayed that somehow God would perform a miracle and find a way for them to be together, and that He'd give him the strength to continue to do what was right if that miracle didn't come.

And Sarah…

Her weekly jaunts into town became almost daily buggy trips. She seemed to have the same need he did to see each other on the streets, to nod at each other in passing, to steal a few spoken moments and words.

Sam leaned against his car door in the parking lot of one of the local restaurants and watched the buggy approach. When it came to a stop beside him, he approached the driver.

"Are you sure about this?"

Benjamin shrugged. "We have to try. Get in."

Sam walked around the horse, and he climbed into the buggy. The irony of the situation did not escape him. He settled onto the seat beside the man who had once been against his presence in this community, and now not only welcomed him but wanted to help.

Benjamin snapped the reins and turned the buggy onto the open road.

"How is Sarah?" Sam could barely wait for Benjamin's reply. He had been on pins and needles since he'd received word that she'd gone into labor.

"The midwife is with her, as well as Rebecca. I am sure all will be well."

Sam's stomach clenched. He wished he could be as confident.

Benjamin laughed. "You would think, the way you pace and worry, that you are the papa. Relax. The women know what they are doing."

Sam tapped his fingers against his knee and looked out over the fields they passed. The harvest complete, the fields stood empty and waiting for the first taste of winter's snow.

It was time for rest, renewal and hope.

Sam's stomach twisted into knots when they turned into the lane leading to the Lapps' farm. As they approached the white clapboard house, his pulse raced and his knees literally knocked together. He hadn't felt so unsettled and unsure of himself since he was a teen.

Benjamin pulled the buggy in front of the barn. Sam hopped out, circled around and met Benjamin as he climbed down.

"I don't know if this is a good idea. Maybe I shouldn't be here, especially today."

Benjamin tilted his head and studied Samuel's face. "Where else should you be on the day Sarah delivers her *boppli?*"

Sam began to pace. "What if this idea of yours doesn't work?"

Benjamin laughed, and the sound startled Sam. He didn't think he'd ever heard the man laugh at anything.

"Where is the brave man we all came to know?" Benjamin asked. "You can capture killers, *ya?* But you cower at the thought of seeing the woman we both know you love?"

"I shouldn't have come. The situation is impossible."

"Nothing is impossible with God." Benjamin put down the reins and gestured with his hand. "I have been praying. I believe God has given me an answer to those prayers."

"What if it doesn't work?"

"Have faith, Samuel. It is in God's hands. Whatever He wants will be. Now let's go inside."

The men had turned toward the house when Benjamin reached out and grabbed his arm. "Wait…"

Sam faced him.

"I think I hear Jacob's voice coming from the barn. It would be best if we spoke to him privately before approaching Rebecca or Sarah."

Sam agreed, and the two men quietly entered the barn.

Jacob's voice drifted from inside one of the far stalls. "I can't believe you are coming to me with this request. Do you know what you are saying? Do you know what it would cost us?"

"Of course I do." Rebecca's voice, timid and filled with tears, reached their ears. "It is all I have thought about… all I have prayed about for weeks. Ever since Samuel came back to town."

Sam knew he should make his presence known and not eavesdrop, but something about the serious tone of the conversation stopped him. Apparently, Benjamin felt the same way. The men glanced at each other and remained still, continuing to listen.

"When Samuel left, everything changed. You know that. Sarah did her best. She is a good and obedient child. She tried to adjust to his absence and commit herself to the Amish life. She did chores, attended services but…"

Rebecca placed her hand on Jacob's arm.

"She can't hide the longing in her eyes from us, Jacob, or her pain. She is still a stranger to herself. She is a stranger even to us. This is *not* our daughter-in-law, Jacob. Not the Sarah we knew."

"What nonsense do you speak? Of course it is."

"No." Rebecca shook her head. "I love her just the same,

but she is different. You know what I say is true. Sarah stayed for us so we could see our grandchild. But her heart…it left with Samuel."

Sam's heart constricted when he heard Rebecca's words.

"That will change with time."

"Will it, Jacob? It has been months, and I have seen no signs of this change. It is even worse now that Samuel has returned."

"Ah, but now she has a daughter. Peter's daughter. Our grandchild. Now she will be happy again."

Sam grinned widely and gave a friendly slap to Benjamin's arm. Sarah had given birth to a baby girl. He wondered if the child had hair the texture of golden silk like her mother. It was all he could do not to run into the house and see for himself.

"Sarah stayed for us, Jacob. She didn't want to hurt us, and with time I believe she has even grown to love us. But asking her to continue to stay for us would be wrong."

Sam's breath caught in his throat. Sarah had missed him. Sarah had had as much trouble letting go of him as he had of her. Maybe there was hope.

"What are you asking of me, Rebecca?" The pain in Jacob's voice was evident in the harshness of his tone.

"I'm asking you to love her, Jacob…as much as she has come to love us. I am asking you to love her enough to let her go…to let her find her heart again…to let her be happy. Hasn't she been through enough? Isn't it selfish to keep her here when we know her heart is elsewhere?"

"But the *boppli*…"

"I know, Jacob. I know." Rebecca's voice choked on sobs. "But she is not happy, and without Samuel I don't believe she ever will be."

As Benjamin and Sam slowly moved forward, they saw Jacob throw his shovel to the ground.

"What you are asking of me is too much. If she leaves, we must shun her. We could not speak to her again. We would have to turn away if we passed her on the street. We would lose Sarah forever, just as we lost Peter, and we would lose our only grandchild. I cannot, Rebecca. I cannot do this."

Rebecca stepped into his arms and held him tightly. "But you will, Jacob. You will let her go because you love her. You will let her go because it is what is best for Sarah."

Sam's throat constricted, and his admiration and affection for this couple grew. He saw the tears and pain etched deeply in Jacob's expression, and it tore at his heart.

"Perhaps there is another way."

Jacob and Rebecca startled at the sound of Benjamin's voice and stepped apart.

Benjamin entered the stall with Sam close behind. "Excuse us for this surprise visit, Bishop, but I believe what I have to say might help."

Jacob blinked in surprise. "Benjamin, what is this about?"

He glanced between the two men. "What are the two of you doing here?"

"Forgive me for the intrusion in what is obviously a private conversation, but I think it is time to speak the truth," Benjamin said.

"What truth?" Rebecca asked.

"The truth that we all lost Sarah the day we lost Peter."

Rebecca gasped, and her hand flew to cover her mouth.

"It's true." Benjamin hurried to finish what he wanted to say. "Do not misunderstand me. We love this Sarah. She is kind and sweet and loving. But she is not the same woman who stepped into the schoolroom that day. She has no memories of that Sarah. She has no memories of us or our way of life. All of us have watched and waited for many months for that woman to return, and she hasn't."

Benjamin stepped forward and placed a comforting hand on Jacob's shoulder. "You know I speak the truth. This is a new woman—in Sarah's body, *ya*—but it is not the Sarah we knew. It is not the woman who was married to Peter. It is not an *Amish* woman."

Jacob opened his mouth to protest, but Benjamin raised his hand to stop him.

"Listen to me, Jacob. She speaks *Englisch* and can only remember some words of our language. She attends our services but can't participate because she does not understand the words of the songs or service. She is not Amish, Jacob. She is *Englisch*. She was born and raised *Englisch*. And after the shooting…" Benjamin looked steadily into Jacob's eyes. "It is the *Englisch* woman who came back to us."

"What are you saying?" Jacob shook his head and stepped away from the three of them, his expression showing how hard he was trying to deny what he knew he had to do. "You are telling me that I should let her go? That I should shun her?"

Benjamin smiled widely. "We do not shun the *Englisch,* Jacob. We befriend them. We welcome them into our homes for visits. We welcome them to join us in our services and gatherings, *ya?*"

A smile creased Rebecca's face as understanding dawned on her. "And this would be acceptable to the community, Benjamin?"

"Forgive me, but I have already taken the liberty to speak to the elders. They agree that the woman residing in Sarah's body is more *Englisch* than Amish. They love her but…" Benjamin shrugged his shoulders. "If God has wiped away her memory, if God has erased the Amish part of her and replaced it with her *Englisch* roots, then it must be God's will, *ya?* And who are we to question God's will?"

All four adults stood in silence as each processed the conversation.

Sam's heart pounded so hard in his chest, he thought it might burst. This was it. The moment of truth. If the bishop and the elders decreed that Sarah was not Amish but *Englisch,* then they would not have to shun her. She could remain an active part of their lives.

Hope filled every pore of his body. Sam bowed his head and prayed. He prayed harder than he had ever prayed before. And he waited.

When an eternity seemed to pass, Rebecca clasped her husband's hand. "Jacob?" Her eyes never left his face as she waited for his answer.

Jacob brushed the tears from his face. "It is true that Sarah was born and raised an *Englisch* child." He turned to face them. "It is also true that since that horrible day in the school, she has no memory of the Amish ways. She does speak the *Englisch* language well, and she struggles to learn ours. It is true that she loves God, but she does not know or understand our *Ordnung,* our Amish rules and laws."

Jacob smiled widely. "What happened to Sarah was God's will, and I will never go against God's will. Sarah is *Englisch.*"

Rebecca flung herself into Jacob's arms, and even though public displays of affection were frowned on in Amish life, this was an exception that all four adults could live with.

Jacob slid his arm around his wife's waist and faced Sam. "Sarah is inside. I am sure she would like you to meet her daughter."

EIGHTEEN

Sarah couldn't tear her eyes away from her daughter. She traced her finger across the baby's soft skin. When she saw the child's lips pucker and suck in sleep, she smiled with joy. She examined the exquisite, perfectly formed little fingers. She grinned at the way her tiny golden tufts of hair stood up at attention, and she wondered if it would remain that way as she grew.

For the hundredth time today, she offered a prayer of thanksgiving to God for blessing her with this tiny miracle.

A light rap sounded on the door. She made sure she was properly covered with the blanket and then called, "Come in."

The door opened.

"Samuel."

The word escaped her lips as a gasp of surprise. Her mouth fell open. Her pulse raced. She must be dreaming. This couldn't be real. Her eyes took in every inch of the apparition standing in front of her. The dark brown hair that still wanted to fall forward across his forehead. The rasp of a day's growth of beard. The dark, compelling eyes that stared back at her with such longing, she didn't think she could draw another breath.

"Can I come in?"

Unable to speak, Sarah simply smiled and nodded.

Sam fell to his knees beside the bed and gazed at the tiny infant held in her mother's arms. The touch of his index finger to the child's fist caused the baby's fingers to startle open, and then they fisted tightly around his finger.

"She's so beautiful, just like her mother."

A warm, tingling sensation flowed through her body when his eyes caught hers.

Thank you, God.

Samuel had come. He was here with her on one of the most important days of her life and was meeting her daughter. Her eyes welled with tears.

"Samuel, what are you doing here?"

"Where else would you have me be?" The baby still clutched his finger, and Samuel seemed hard-pressed to claim it back. He glanced up at her, and the look of awe and joy in his eyes stole her breath away.

Sarah glanced at the open doorway and then back at Samuel. "Do Jacob and Rebecca know you are here?"

"Yes, of course. They are in the barn with Benjamin. They gave me their blessing and sent me in to see you."

Sarah's mouth fell open, and for a moment she didn't have any words. When she finally found her voice, she could no longer hide the tears that flowed down her face.

"I don't understand. Gave you their blessing? What does that mean?"

Sam grinned and placed the index finger that wasn't being held in the baby's fisted grip against her lips. "It means God has answered our prayers, *lieb*. He in His infinite wisdom devised a way for us to be together, and I will fall on my knees in thanksgiving every day for the rest of my life."

He replaced his finger with his lips in a kiss so sweet,

so tender, that she thought she'd never forget this moment of absolute joy.

This wasn't an apparition. This was real. The feel of his touch on her skin. The taste of his kiss on her mouth. Samuel was here, with her, on one of the most important days of her life. He was crooning over her baby. He was smiling down into her eyes and stroking her cheek. She didn't understand it all, but at that moment it didn't matter.

"We have much to talk about, Samuel."

"We do, *lieb*. But we also have time…lots and lots of time."

Why had Samuel suddenly appeared at her door? How could he possibly have Jacob and Rebecca's blessing? But Sam had proved himself to be a man of his word. For now, just seeing him was enough.

Overwhelming waves of emotion gripped her. Tears tracked down her cheeks like streams escaping a dam. But they were good tears, happy tears. For what could make this day more perfect than to be sharing it with her newborn daughter and gazing at the man she loved with all her heart?

She swiped the back of her hand against her face. *Must be hormones setting off these endless tears.*

Sarah quietly watched Samuel interact with her daughter.

"Hello, little one," he whispered in the deep, caring voice she had come to love. His tender expression as he gazed down at the baby touched Sarah's heart. When he glanced up, his eyes glistened. Hmm. *Was he having a surge of hormones, too?*

They spent the next few hours sitting, the three of them—talking, laughing, enjoying their first day together.

Rebecca had come into the room twice. Once just to

see if anyone needed anything, and then hours later with a tray laden with sandwiches, fruit and tea.

Samuel took the time to repeat the conversation that had occurred in the barn. He told her that Benjamin had approached the elders, and after several hours of deliberation, they came up with the solution that everyone believed was the right one, one all could happily live with.

Once again Samuel fell to his knee beside Sarah's bed. This time he wasn't focused on the sleeping child in her arms. This time he clasped her hand and looked deeply into her eyes.

"I love you, Sarah. I think I have been in love with you from the very first moment you opened your eyes in that hospital room. You were so vulnerable and lost and frightened." He grinned widely. "But you were also strong, resilient and determined." He drew her hand to his lips and kissed her palm. "From the moment I looked into those beautiful blue eyes of yours, I knew my life was about to change."

Samuel reached into his pocket, extended his hand and opened it.

Nestled softly on his palm was a simple silver band with a small diamond stone. "I know the Amish do not exchange wedding rings. But neither of us are Amish, Sarah. We are *Englisch,* and I would be honored if you would accept this ring and agree to be my wife."

Sarah stared at the ring.

Was this really happening? Had God truly answered her prayers?

She smiled such a wide grin that her face hurt. "Yes, Samuel. I will wear your ring. I will be your wife."

He slipped the band on her finger and clasped her hand in his.

"The repairs on my house are almost finished. I think

you will like the house, Sarah. It has a large kitchen and lots of windows for light. There is a stone fireplace in the living room, and there are four bedrooms upstairs."

"Four? Are you planning for us to have several children, Samuel?"

Sarah almost laughed out loud at the embarrassed flush that colored his neck.

"Would that be acceptable to you?" He looked at her earnestly.

"More than acceptable, my love. I want to fill our lives and our home with many, many children."

"I do have one thing I must talk to you about."

She was surprised by the seriousness of his tone, and she waited for him to continue.

"I am a cop, Sarah. I've been a cop my entire adult life. I don't know any other way of life." He gazed deeply in her eyes. "But I'm willing to try to be something else. A farmer, maybe. Or perhaps I can learn woodworking. I did a decent job on that table I finished."

Sarah cupped his face in her hand. "I do not know Samuel the farmer. Nor have I met Samuel the woodworker. I only know the man I met and the man I love with all my heart...and that man is a cop. A very good cop, I might add. And I wouldn't want him to try to be anything that he is not."

"Are you absolutely certain? I want you to be happy, Sarah. I do not want you to have any regrets."

"No regrets. But one ironclad rule."

He arched an eyebrow in question.

"There are never to be guns in reach or sight of the children. Not ever."

"I promise." Samuel leaned forward and sealed the promise with a kiss.

"Speaking of children," Sam said, turning his attention to the sleeping infant in her mother's arms. "What have you decided to name this precious one?" Sam gently stroked the wisps of golden locks that continued to stand straight up in the air.

"I don't know yet," Sarah replied. "I've been holding her for the last few hours and trying to decide what name best suits her."

"I know what we should call her."

We? Did he say "we"?

Sarah's heart felt like a bird thrashing in her chest. The three of them were going to be a family. She didn't believe it was possible for a person to be so happy.

"Faith." Sam's eyes locked with hers. "Let's name her Faith."

When Sam's lips touched hers in a passionate kiss full of promises for the future, Sarah knew he was right. Faith was the perfect name. Sarah had complete faith that they had a long and happy future stretching out in front of them. Their future was in God's hands—and God was good.

EPILOGUE

Jacob snapped the reins, and the horse and buggy cleared the curve and approached the white house on the hill.

"What time will Samuel be joining us?" He glanced over at his passenger and smiled. "Rebecca has baked a fresh apple pie, and she will not allow anyone near it until Samuel arrives."

Sarah grinned. "He won't be long. He got called over to the Millers' farm. Someone tampered with his fencing, and his cows are scattered up and down the road."

Jacob chuckled. "That must be a sight. Cars and cows on the same roads. Perhaps the cows will win, and the *Englisch* drivers will go away—permanently."

Sarah laughed. "You know you don't mean a word of that, Jacob. The tourists provide an excellent market for your produce and Rebecca's pies."

Jacob pulled up to the hitching post.

"I know. I know." He waved his hand dismissively. "But I cannot help but wish I could steer my buggy into town without horns blasting and my horse being skittish each time the cars rev their engines or rush past."

Jacob jumped out of the buggy and tied the reins to the post.

"*Kumm, kumm,* everyone has been waiting." Rebecca

beckoned to Sarah and stretched out her arms. "Let me have the *boppli*."

Sarah smiled as she handed her sleeping daughter down into her grandmother's waiting arms. Jacob came around and offered her a hand getting out of the buggy.

Sarah followed the two of them to the grove, where picnic tables covered by white tablecloths dotted the horizon. Even from this distance, Sarah could recognize most of her neighbors already socializing.

"Sarah, Sarah!" William and Mary raced across the lawn in her direction. "Did you bring any cookies with you?"

Sarah laughed. "Get the basket off the floor of the backseat of the buggy. Carry it over to the table, and I will let each of you sample one cookie apiece."

The children dashed off.

Benjamin followed them with his gaze. "They should not be asking you for cookies, Sarah. I will speak with them."

"Nonsense, Benjamin. They are children. Let them be."

"Only if I am also allowed to sample the wares."

Sarah's eyes widened with surprise, and she laughed. "Well, Benjamin, if I didn't know any better, I would swear you are just a big kid yourself."

The sound of her daughter's voice caught and held Sarah's attention.

"Looks like someone just woke up from her nap."

Faith squirmed in her grandmother's arms and tried to get down.

"No, precious. If I put you on the ground, you will get dirt all over your hands. Let's sit down at the table, and Grandmom will fix you something to eat."

A car approached, kicking up dirt and dust as it sped closer.

Jacob shook his head from side to side. "There's something about cars and speed that appeals to Samuel, but I am afraid I will never understand."

"I understand it, Jacob. Samuel doesn't want to miss Faith's first birthday party. Why don't you and Benjamin join the others? I will wait here for Samuel, and we'll be over in just a moment."

The warmth of the sun beat on Sarah's face, and the light breeze ruffled the wisps of hair framing her cheeks. Sounds of laughter and conversations wafted on the air. The party was in full swing, and from her vantage point she could see her daughter basking in the love and attention.

Sam kissed her on the back of the neck, and Sarah startled and squealed.

"You saw me coming, *lieb*. How could I startle you?"

She wrapped her arm around his waist, and he encircled hers. "I was so lost in the beauty of the day, I didn't hear you approach."

As they walked toward the others, Samuel asked, "Have I missed anything? They haven't sung or cut the cake yet, have they?"

Sarah grinned. "You haven't missed a thing. We just got here."

Samuel nodded, happy that he'd made it in time.

"I can't believe it's Faith's first birthday. It seems like only yesterday we were sitting together in this very house and trying to decide on a name for our daughter."

Our daughter.

A flash of warmth and love flooded her being. Samuel had always treated Faith as his daughter from that very first day, and the child adored him.

"Have you told them?" Samuel asked.

"Without you? How could you think such a thing?"

Samuel's smile widened. "Let's tell them now." He steered her toward the gathering of friends and family.

After pleasantries were exchanged, Samuel clasped Sarah's hand and pulled her toward him.

"This is a very special day," Samuel said. "Faith is one year old today."

Everyone cheered and fussed over the child.

"It has been a good year, *ya?*" Benjamin asked. "Good weather. Good harvest. Good friends. And now time to eat good food!"

Everyone laughed as he reached for a chicken leg and Rebecca shooed his hand away.

Rebecca tilted her head and stared hard at Sarah and Samuel. Then a grin broke out on her face, and she clapped her hands together. "You have news, *ya?*"

Her words silenced the group, and all eyes turned toward them.

Sarah smiled up into her husband's face. It was a good face. Strong features. Strong jaw. Eyes that shone with intelligence—and love.

Her heart overflowed with emotion. God had brought such blessings into her life. Her smile widened so much, she thought it would no longer fit her face.

"You tell them," she whispered.

"Tell us what?" Jacob asked.

"They don't have to say a word. It's written all over their faces, Jacob. Can't you see?" Rebecca rushed forward, Faith wrapped in her arms and clinging to her neck. "Faith is going to have a little brother or sister, *ya?*"

Sarah smiled and nodded. The crowd cheered and congratulated them.

"That is great news," Benjamin said. "Now let's celebrate by eating."

Laughter filled the air as friends and neighbors resumed talking while filling their plates.

Sarah's gaze drifted to the horizon. From this distance, Peter's headstone was a mere shadow on the rise. A twinge of sadness touched her heart that no memories of the man had returned. But the sadness was immediately replaced with happy thoughts. She had a pretty good guess now what he must have looked like. She saw glimpses of him every time she looked into her daughter's face, and felt nothing but fondness and gratitude toward the man.

Sarah could feel the warmth of Samuel's breath on the back of her neck.

"Penny for your thoughts."

"I was thinking what a perfect day today is."

He spun her around and smiled down at her. His lips brushed hers softly and tenderly. She could smell the fresh, clean scent of mint and could taste a trace of coffee on his lips.

"Now it is a perfect day," he whispered.

Sarah reached up and cupped his face with her hand. She smiled into his eyes. Without a word, she stood on tiptoe and kissed him back, long and passionately, expressing all the love and joy her heart could hold. "Now, my love, it is a perfect day."

Samuel's eyes glistened. "How did I ever find someone as wonderful as you?"

"I was gift wrapped in bandages and express-delivered to your care by God," Sarah replied.

Samuel laughed. "That you were. And I will be forever grateful to the good Lord for such a wonderful gift." He clasped her hand and tugged her toward the picnic tables.

"Speaking of gifts, Faith is waiting for us to open hers. Let's go and help our daughter eat her cake."

Sarah offered a silent prayer of thanksgiving as she crossed the lawn to join her family and friends. God makes all things good…and Sarah's life was good, indeed.

* * * * *

*If you enjoyed this story by Diane Burke,
be sure to check out the other books
this month from Love Inspired Suspense!*

Dear Reader,

By the time you read this book, almost two years have passed from its inception to the time it appeared on the shelves. This book deals with the underlying theme of adoption and self-identity. Sarah is born in the *Englisch* world but raised in the Amish. When tragic circumstances develop, the main question raised is: What constitutes family? Do you belong to the one you were born into, or do you belong in the family that raised you?

While I explored my feelings on this subject through the lives of my characters during the writing of this book, I had no idea how very close to home those questions would hit. To my ultimate surprise, in April 2012, I received a certified letter that changed my life. A child I had given up for adoption more than forty years ago had found me. The ripples of that moment have stretched out and touched all my family and friends in many ways. God has blessed me, and I will be forever thankful.

So anyone who has read my biography in prior books, please consider this a disclaimer. I have THREE sons, five grandchildren and three step-grandchildren.

And like Sarah, my long-lost son and I have found a way to bridge both the biological and adoptive worlds and now enjoy the blessings of a wonderful and much larger extended family.

I am always happy to hear from my readers. You can reach me at diane@dianeburkeauthor.com.

Blessings and thank you for sharing my joy,

Diane Burke

Questions for Discussion

1. In the opening scenes of *Hidden in Plain View,* Sarah is faced with a terrible tragedy. Have you been faced with the loss of a loved one? How did you cope with your grief?

2. Due to her injuries, Sarah had to deal with returning to a world she couldn't remember, but the one thing she hadn't forgotten was her belief in God and her ability to pray. How important a role do you think prayer played in Sarah's life? How important a role does prayer play in your own life?

3. Sarah, a pregnant widow with amnesia, finds herself drawn to Samuel, the strong, quiet but troubled man who is charged with her protection. She experienced guilt for harboring feelings for a man who wasn't her deceased husband, even though she was widowed and had no memories of him. Guilt can be fruit of a poisonous tree. How does a belief in God help free us from the heavy burden of guilt we might carry for acts of our own?

4. Samuel finds this particular job stressful because he must return to his Amish roots, which he had left as a teenager. In what ways has Sam changed since he moved into the *Englisch* world? In what ways are his Amish roots still evident in his life and his character?

5. Benjamin, an Amish neighbor and friend of the Lapp family, is very much opposed to Samuel and his role in Sarah's life. Why? How does Benjamin change over time, and why do you think he did?

6. A strong underlying theme in this book is the power of love—love of child, love of family, love of each other, love of God. How did the characters in this book best express their love? How do you show your love for the people in your life on a daily basis?

7. Rebecca plays a prominent role in Sarah and Samuel's relationship. Why do you think she made the decisions she did? Do you think you might have made the same decisions under similar circumstances? How did she grow and change as a Christian?

8. Sarah helped Samuel face his past and deal with his pain and loss. Is there anyone in your life suffering right now? How could you reach out but do it in a Christian, loving way?

9. Benjamin's son has a pivotal role in this story. The little boy used a slingshot to achieve his goals. What biblical hero also used a slingshot, and what similarities do you see between both stories? What is the slingshot you may be challenged to use in your life?

10. Most of the characters in this story make sacrificial decisions that impact another's life. How did you feel about those decisions? Would you have made the same decisions if you were faced with similar problems? If not, what else might you have done?

11. What was your favorite scene in this story and why?

12. Which character affected you the most and why?

13. What spiritual impact, if any, did this book have on you?

REQUEST YOUR FREE BOOKS!

2 FREE RIVETING INSPIRATIONAL NOVELS
PLUS 2 FREE MYSTERY GIFTS

Love Inspired®
SUSPENSE

YES! Please send me 2 FREE Love Inspired® Suspense novels and my 2 FREE mystery gifts (gifts are worth about $10). After receiving them, if I don't wish to receive any more books, I can return the shipping statement marked "cancel." If I don't cancel, I will receive 4 brand-new novels every month and be billed just $4.49 per book in the U.S. or $4.99 per book in Canada. That's a savings of at least 22% off the cover price. It's quite a bargain! Shipping and handling is just 50¢ per book in the U.S. and 75¢ per book in Canada.* I understand that accepting the 2 free books and gifts places me under no obligation to buy anything. I can always return a shipment and cancel at any time. Even if I never buy another book, the two free books and gifts are mine to keep forever.

123/323 IDN FVWV

Name _____ (PLEASE PRINT)

Address _____ Apt. #

City _____ State/Prov. _____ Zip/Postal Code

Signature (if under 18, a parent or guardian must sign)

Mail to the **Harlequin®** Reader Service:
IN U.S.A.: P.O. Box 1867, Buffalo, NY 14240-1867
IN CANADA: P.O. Box 609, Fort Erie, Ontario L2A 5X3

**Are you a subscriber to Love Inspired Suspense
and want to receive the larger-print edition?
Call 1-800-873-8635 or visit www.ReaderService.com.**

* Terms and prices subject to change without notice. Prices do not include applicable taxes. Sales tax applicable in N.Y. Canadian residents will be charged applicable taxes. Offer not valid in Quebec. This offer is limited to one order per household. Not valid for current subscribers to Love Inspired Suspense books. All orders subject to credit approval. Credit or debit balances in a customer's account(s) may be offset by any other outstanding balance owed by or to the customer. Please allow 4 to 6 weeks for delivery. Offer available while quantities last.

Your Privacy—The Harlequin® Reader Service is committed to protecting your privacy. Our Privacy Policy is available online at www.ReaderService.com or upon request from the Harlequin Reader Service.
We make a portion of our mailing list available to reputable third parties that offer products we believe may interest you. If you prefer that we not exchange your name with third parties, or if you wish to clarify or modify your communication preferences, please visit us at www.ReaderService.com/consumerchoice or write to us at Harlequin Reader Service Preference Service, P.O. Box 9062, Buffalo, NY 14269. Include your complete name and address.

LIS13

Detective Melody Zachary halted abruptly at the sight of her office door of the Sagebrush Youth Center cracked open. Unease slithered down her spine. She'd locked the door last night when she left the center.

Pushing back her suit jacket, she withdrew her weapon. She pushed the door wide with the toe of her boot. Stepping inside the room, she reached for the overhead light switch and froze.

A shadow moved.

Not a shadow. A man.

Dressed from head to toe in black. Black gloves, black ski mask....

Palming her piece in both hands, she aimed her weapon. "Halt! Police!"

The intruder dove straight at her. She didn't have time to react, before he slammed into her chest, knocking her backward against the wall. Her head smacked hard, sending pain slicing through her brain.

The man bolted through the open doorway and disappeared.

Melody pushed away from the wall. For a moment her off-balance equilibrium sent the world spinning.

The exit door at the end of the hall banged shut. He was escaping.

Melody chased after the intruder. Out on the sidewalk, she searched for the trespasser. Sagebrush Boulevard was empty.

Holstering her piece and pulling her jacket closed, she retraced her steps and entered Sagebrush Youth Center's single-story brick building.

She stopped in her office doorway. The place had been ransacked. The filing cabinet had been emptied, the files strewn all over. The pictures of her family had been knocked off the desk.

A sense of violation cramped her chest. She was used to investigating this sort of vandalism, not being the victim herself.

Yanking her cell phone out of her purse, she dialed the Sagebrush police dispatch and reported the crime.

For the past several years, a crime wave had terrorized the citizens of Sagebrush. The mastermind behind the crime syndicate was a faceless, nameless entity that even the thugs who worked for "The Boss" feared.

A short time later, the center's front door opened. A small dog with his black nose pressed to the ground entered. Melody recognized the beagle as Sherlock, part of the K-9 unit. A harness attached to a leash led to the handsome man at the other end. Melody blinked.

What were narcotics detective Parker Adams and his K-9 partner doing here?

To find out, pick up SCENT OF DANGER
wherever Love Inspired Suspense books are sold.
Available May 2013

Love Inspired®
SUSPENSE
RIVETING INSPIRATIONAL ROMANCE

Eric Lander hated to be tied down...

But when Sarah Trask, the woman he'd left months ago, came to him for help solving a very personal murder, saying no wasn't even an option. Especially once he learned she was pregnant with his child...

Running from the law through the Rocky Mountains after being wrongly accused about his role in the killing wasn't exactly how Eric planned on absorbing—or celebrating—the big news. Yet they had no other choice. Now, with the beautiful rancher and their unborn baby counting on him for protection, Eric found himself both excited and terrified by the idea of "family." He knew he'd be a good father—if only he could keep them all alive to prove it.

FUGITIVE
by
SHIRLEE McCOY

HEROES
for HIRE

**Available May 2013
wherever books are sold.**

www.LoveInspiredBooks.com

LIS44537

Will You Marry Me?

Bold widow Johanna Yoder stuns Roland Byler when she asks
him to be her husband. To Johanna, it seems very sensible that
they marry. She has two children, he has a son. Why shouldn't
their families become one? But the widower has never forgotten
his long-ago love for her; it was his foolish mistake that split
them apart. This could be a fresh start for both of them—until
she reveals she wants a marriage of convenience only. It's up to
Roland to woo the stubborn Johanna and convince her to accept
him as her groom in her home and in her heart.

Hannah's Daughters

Johanna's Bridegroom

by

Emma Miller

Available May 2013

www.LoveInspiredBooks.com

LI8781